Chipo waited until he was sure the other children and Tortu were asleep, and then wriggled his way to Dede's end of the bunk. Halfway there he found Dede was doing the same thing!

"Chipo," Dede breathed in the world's smallest whisper, "what's wrong with those kids? There's something funny about this place, isn't there?"

Clapping Dede on the back would have made way too much noise, but that's what Chipo wanted to do. "Dede, you are a lot cleverer than you look," he whispered. "You're right. And that's why we're getting out of here!"

Also available by Nicola Davies,
and published by
Random House Children's Books:

A Girl Called Dog

Nicola Davies

RUBBISH TOWN HERO

CORGI BOOKS

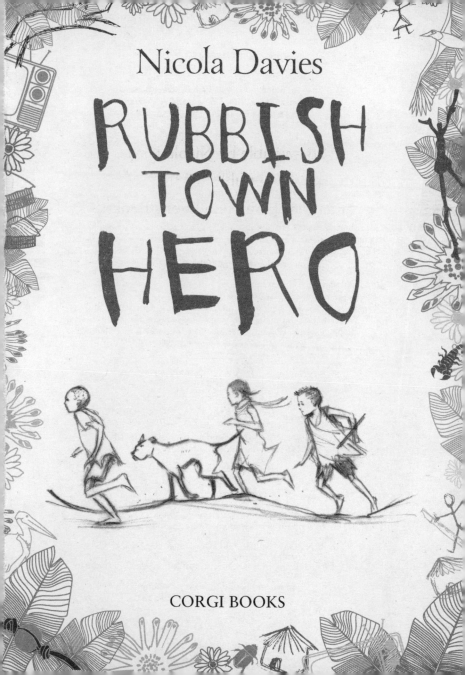

RUBBISH TOWN HERO
A CORGI BOOK 978 0 552 56302 4

First published in Great Britain by Corgi Books,
an imprint of Random House Children's Books
A Random House Group Company

This edition published 2012

1 3 5 7 9 10 8 6 4 2

The Random House Group Limited supports the Forest Stewardship Council
(FSC®), the leading international forest certification organization. Our books
carrying the FSC label are printed on FSC®-certified paper. FSC is the only
forest certification scheme endorsed by the leading environmental organizations,
including Greenpeace. Our paper procurement policy can be found at
www.**randomhouse**.co.uk/environment.

MIX
Paper from
responsible sources
FSC® C016897

Set in Adobe Garamond Pro 14/20.5pt

Corgi Books are published by Random House Children's Books,
61–63 Uxbridge Road, London W5 5SA

www.**randomhouse**.co.uk
www.**kids**at**randomhouse**.co.uk
www.**totallyrandombooks**.co.uk

Addresses for companies within The Random House Group Limited can
be found at: www.randomhouse.co.uk/offices.htm

THE RANDOM HOUSE GROUP Limited Reg. No. 954009

A CIP catalogue record for this book is available from the British Library.

Printed and bound in Great Britain by
CPI Group (UK), Croydon, CR0 4YY

For Joseph and Gabriel
with love

Chapter 1

At first Chipo couldn't believe his eyes. It seemed impossible that something so big and valuable was still left on the Old Dump, where all the rubbish had been searched and sifted time after time. Yet there it was – a TV, a small corner of its blue-grey screen peeping through the grey fragments of trash, like a milky eye looking right at him. He could trade a TV like that for a big piece of tin roof – a roof good enough to keep a person dry when it rained and shady when it didn't.

Chipo knew he should pull it out right now and add it to the rest of his finds to give to his boss, Papa Fudu, who owned the dump. But Papa Fudu wouldn't pay him what the TV was really worth; he would just pat Chipo on the head and give him an extra ration of food. No, Chipo decided, this was too good a chance to miss; he would keep the TV for himself.

But finding a way to keep the TV wasn't easy. First he had to hide it so that the other boys picking over the rubbish, watched over by Papa Fudu's grumpy son, Owiti, wouldn't find it. Then he had to get back into the dump at night to fetch it. If he hid it well enough to keep it from Owiti and the boys, how would he himself find it again in the dark?

Chipo had to think quick, move fast. He smiled to himself: he was good at those things.

He glanced about him, at the lines of skinny,

raggedy kids with bulging sacks on their backs. Their shadows slanted behind them in the evening light, like long-legged tortoises. Dede was the closest, but Dede always paid more attention to playing the tin whistle he kept strung round his neck than to his job. He was doing that now, standing on tiptoe as if he wanted the notes of his tune to carry him away. None of the other children *seemed* to be looking Chipo's way, but you couldn't be too sure.

Chipo shuffled his feet to push a little wave of rubbish over the peeping eye of the screen. Then he yelled at the top of his lungs, "Scorpion! Scorpion! Stay back!"

Dede's whistle dropped from his lips and he scuttled backwards. "Where? Where? Where?" he panted.

"Here!" said Chipo, stabbing the ground a couple of metres in front of him with his stick.

"Right – here – under – my – stick."

Several pairs of eyes focused on the end of
Chipo's stick as it stabbed into the rubbish,
jabbing the imaginary scorpion and covering
the TV up still further.

"Eeeiii!" squealed Dede. "I see it! I see
it!" And he pointed, still squealing, to where
Chipo's stick cut deep into the trash.

"There," said Chipo, giving one last extra-
hard stab. "It's dead."

Dede peered at the spot; he was an especially
small child, just the sort that died quite easily
from a scorpion sting. "Are you sure?" he said.

"Yes, but there could be others," Chipo
replied. He liked Dede, and didn't want to
scare him, but this time it couldn't be helped.
"I'll mark the place," he announced, "so we
know to keep away and stay safe."

"Thanks, Chipo," said Dede, smiling his
sweet smile.

Chipo felt bad; Dede was so like him, really – a child without any adults to look out for him – and he couldn't even think quick or move fast. Chipo smiled back and told himself he would do something for Dede to make up for this lie; maybe he'd give him some of what he'd found that day, because staring at the sky playing his whistle, Dede wasn't going to find much that would please Papa Fudu.

Chipo marked the scorpion spot with a flag made from a long plastic slat from a window blind and a white polythene carrier bag. He stuck it firmly into the rubbish at his feet, so that he could find this spot when he came back in the dark. He looked around and saw Owiti, big scowling Owiti, with his long knobbly legs, standing at the top of a hill of rubbish, staring at him. Silhouetted against the sky, Owiti reminded Chipo of a maribou stork – the ugliest, meanest bird in all of Africa. He was probably thinking of a way to do Chipo some harm, as usual. Chipo wasn't sure why Owiti hated him so much; maybe because of the way Fudu always praised Chipo's hard work. *Maybe*, he thought, smiling to himself, *because I'm fast and he's slow*. Well, Owiti wouldn't spoil his plans this time.

When it grew too dark to work, Papa Fudu came in his truck to fetch them.

He slapped each child on the back as they climbed into the truck, feeling the contents of their sacks. "What you got for me tonight, eh, boys?" he laughed. "Treasure and riches? Or just a load of old junk?"

He slapped Owiti's back too as he climbed into the truck. "Hope you're learning your trade as well as Chipo already knows it!" he said.

Owiti just scowled, and Papa Fudu laughed

again, like a car engine trying to start; then he swung himself into the driver's seat, and the truck lumbered and bumped over the trash mountains towards the tall metal gates of the Old Dump.

Chipo held onto the side of the bouncing truck and stared out at the trees and bushes that sprouted in the grey sea of old rubbish. He tried to fix some landmarks in his mind to help him find his way back in the dark.

"What are you up to, Chipo?" Owiti's voice rasped close to his ear. "You better not be stealing from my dad. I didn't see any scorpion. I'm not as stupid as the others."

Chipo went on staring out at the passing rubbish-scape (two more bushes, one shaped just like a dog), pretending he didn't care what Owiti said to him.

"No, you're not *as* stupid," he replied,

sounding as bored as he could. "You're *more* stupid. If you weren't stupid," he went on, "then you'd know a scorpion is *small* and you were too far away to see it."

Owiti ground his teeth in anger and slowly trod on Chipo's foot. Chipo didn't flinch; he didn't even look at Owiti – he wouldn't give that satisfaction to his enemy. Out of the corner of his eye he saw that some of the other boys were watching the two of them to see if there would be another fight: Owiti and Chipo had fought each other a few times now. Owiti, being much bigger, always won, but Chipo never admitted he'd lost, which just made Owiti more angry. This time the boys were disappointed. The truck stopped with a shudder, jerking Chipo and Owiti apart. Papa Fudu locked the big gates behind them and they rolled on to Rubbish Town.

Chapter 2

Rubbish Town was a town made of rubbish.
Houses made of flattened-out tins or cardboard
or strips of plastic bag stuck together.
Everything, and everybody, in Rubbish Town
had been thrown away at least once.

At one end of town was the Old Dump and
at the other was the New Dump. Trucks full
of new rubbish arrived at the New Dump all
the time, day and night. New rubbish was a
treasure trove: it contained all manner of riches
– food, clothes, fridges, cookers, DVDs, toys,

bikes, everything! Chipo dreamed of being allowed to search through a big, smelly, sticky load of it. But the gates to the New Dump were guarded by men with guns. You had to know the right people to work on the New Dump, and be big and tough enough to fight for anything you found.

Papa Fudu had worked on the New Dump when he was a young man. His nose was crooked and his cheeks were scarred, showing how hard he'd once fought for his place at the very front, where the rubbish tipped, fresh and full of promise, off the back of the lorries. Now he stuck to the Old Dump, and his wife and two eldest sons took his old spot on the New Dump, where the freshest trash was unloaded.

The story was that Fudu had won the Old Dump in a fight. He'd mended all the fences so that no one but him and his gangs of sharp-eyed boys could get in there to find metal, wood and plastic to sell for good money.

"She's slow and steady, that Old Dump," Fudu told everyone. "Just right for a slow old guy like me."

But everyone knew Papa Fudu was still a fighter, as sly as a jackal and as dangerous as a scorpion. No one really believed that "slow and steady" was enough for him. Fudu had other, bigger plans for that dump, for sure, but nobody could say exactly what.

Whatever they were, everyone knew Owiti wasn't pleased about them. Owiti was always grumbling about the Old Dump and how he wanted to work on the New Dump with his big brothers, but Fudu said he wasn't allowed to until he'd "learned his trade". So all day Owiti took his bad temper out on the boys in Fudu's search gangs, kicking and slapping them – all much smaller than him – for the slightest thing. Fudu knew about it, but perhaps he thought that kicking people smaller than you was part of Owiti's training. The only real difference between father and son was that Fudu was a bully who smiled and Owiti wasn't.

Papa Fudu had a lot to smile about. It was clear from his round tummy that he never went hungry, and his house was one of the grandest in Rubbish Town. Only the bosses of the New Dump had homes with more rooms. Chipo looked at Fudu's house with a kind of awe, and told himself that one day he would build one just like it: *two* rooms, *each* with a tin roof, a lean-to kitchen on the side, and *three* different saucepans, with something cooking in all of them.

Papa Fudu's house had a generator that ran electric lights and – most wonderful for

Chipo and the other boys – a TV. Sometimes, at the end of the day, if Fudu was in an especially good mood, he'd let the boys watch it. Cartoons were Chipo's favourite: he rolled around on the floor laughing when Jerry mouse defeated Tom cat *again*; he dreamed of being a superhero – Spider-man or Batman, perhaps, or his favourite, Powerbolt. Powerbolt was a superhero who could fly without wings and was so strong he could lift elephants and stop a truck with one hand. He was always saving people from danger. In one episode that Chipo always loved, which was on TV time after time, Powerbolt saved the whole of Africa from a plague of giant monsters called dinosaurs. Just thinking about it made Chipo feel bigger and stronger.

But tonight the generator wasn't working. The TV was dead, and Fudu sat behind his

big table in the light of a kerosene lantern. A
spring balance dangled from the beam above,
to weigh whatever plastic, wood or metal the
boys had found. Fudu recorded each boy's tally
and paid him for it at the end of the month
when the big bales of plastic, wood and metal
were sold. But no one ever got even half of
what they were owed. Smiling his big smile,
Fudu kept most of the money for himself.

So although Chipo only used his pay to buy
dried beans or a bag of rice, well before the
end of the month it always ran out. Now, still
a week away from payday, Chipo was glad that
Fudu also paid his boys in food that his family
had found in the New Dump. But to get the
best of it you had to please Papa Fudu.

As usual, the food-pay was piled in a basket
beside Fudu's desk. Chipo took a good look at
what he might get today: the best items were

two sandwiches, still in their packet, with just
one bite taken out of one and a bit of mould
on the other, and an almost full tin of beans;
the worst were a very small, very black banana,
and four biscuits with splodges of what might
have been oil, but could have been something
much worse.

"OK, boys," said Fudu. "Time to show me what you've got!"

The boys lined up, silently shoving and jostling each other for position. Chipo usually went close to the back; that way, by the time Chipo collected his pay, Owiti would be eating his dinner or doing chores for his mother, too busy to cause trouble. But Chipo had a lot to do tonight so he needed to be first. The other boys knew how hard he could kick, so he got in right at the front of the line. But then, at the last moment, little Dede wriggled through in front of him and stepped up to the desk! For a moment Chipo felt cross; then he remembered his unspoken promise to Dede, and let him push in without a word.

Chipo noticed that Dede was even skinner this week than last, so you could count all his ribs; the only bit of him that was thriving was his hair, which stood up on his little head like a brush. He had arrived, as most lone children seemed to do, out of nowhere, at the end of the last rainy season, and somehow persuaded Fudu to employ him. He never found much of any value, and Fudu was coming to the end of his patience with him. All the same, Dede stepped forward hopefully to show his finds.

Papa Fudu's face screwed up like a gathering thundercloud. "I pay for plastic, for metal, for wood," he growled, counting the items off on his fat fingers, "but all you have brought me, *again*, are pretty pieces of broken pot!"

Dede was going to get fired, Chipo just knew it. He decided to do something. He slipped a coil of wire out of his own pack and cleared his throat.

"Excuse me," he said. "Papa Fudu, I think Dede dropped this." He put the coil down

amongst the pieces of pottery that Dede had
collected.

"Hmmm," said Papa Fudu. "Copper wire.
Very valuable." He looked from Dede to
Chipo and back again. "You are a very lucky
boy, Dede." He pointed to the black-splodged
biscuits. "Take them and I will add the wire to
your tally. But tomorrow is your last chance.
Now go!"

Dede backed away, as if he'd been pushed
by Fudu's pointing finger. He smiled quickly at
Chipo and raced off.

Chipo stepped forward and emptied his sack
onto the desk – two bent saucepan lids, about
thirty short sections of electrical wire, and
twelve flattened plastic bottles. None of which
Papa Fudu would pay him properly for, which
made him feel a bit better about planning to
keep the TV for himself.

"See this, Owiti?" Fudu said, turning to where his son lurked in the shadows by the stove, arms full of firewood. "This is good work. Aluminium in those pan lids, copper in the cable, and we'll add the plastic to your weekly total, Chipo." He pointed to the food. "You are my best worker, Chipo. Take the sandwiches."

Chipo felt Owiti's eyes glaring at him as he snatched up the triangle-shaped box. But he didn't even bother to look round at the boy. What did Owiti matter today, when he, Chipo, was almost a superhero, with food for supper and a TV to trade? He raced off through the Rubbish Town crowds and out into the dark beyond. Unlike Dede, Chipo had someone with whom to share good news – his sister.

Chapter 3

Chipo walked alone on the road near the gates
to the Old Dump. The procession of dustbin
lorries churned the dust into the air, so that
their headlights looked as though they were
cutting through a thick fog. Chipo pulled his
T-shirt over his mouth and nose so he could
breathe. Then, when he was sure he was alone
in the perfect blackness between lorries, he
scrambled up the bank beside the road.

On the other side of the bank, the ground
was bare and burned, blasted full of holes

and craters where bombs and mines had gone off in the war. Chipo picked his way over hummocks and mounds and around holes. About a hundred metres from the road, he disappeared into a crater, like a stone dropped into a black pool.

At the bottom of the crater was a circle of yellow candlelight, and at the edge of the circle sat Chipo's sister, Gentle.

She was smaller than Chipo, and never seemed to grow much. She'd been born with a split in her top lip and the roof of her mouth – what people call a cleft palate, although Chipo and Gentle didn't know that. They just called it a "split face". It made eating difficult for Gentle, and she often got sick. But she was tough, and never complained. All day she worked, washing out old rubbish bags in the river on the edge of the New Dump, and now she was counting her earnings by candlelight – one penny for every hundred bags she washed.

She grinned up at him. "Hello, Chipo!" she said, although it sounded more like "Hewo, Theepo".

Chipo hardly noticed the funny way Gentle talked, or how her face looked, but other people did. They laughed at the weird way she spoke. They said cruel things, even threw stones. So Chipo and Gentle lived out here, where there weren't any people. When Gentle went to work she wrapped her face in a bandage and talked as little as possible. All the same, Chipo worried about her and was always glad to see she'd come home safe.

Gentle opened her hand to show the new coins in her palm. "Five more pennies," she said proudly, then tipped them into the rusty little tin box where she kept her most precious things: all her savings; a tiny doll made of sticks, with a rag dress; and a blue glass bead that Gentle said had been their mother's, although Chipo wasn't sure that was true.

"Five more pennies!" she said again. "Soon I'll have enough to go to Happy Split-face Land. And I can be happy and we can go to school."

Chipo didn't say what he thought, which was: *There's no such place*, or, *We don't need to go to school*. It was no good, because Gentle would just stick her nose in the air and say what she always said:

"I *know* there is such a place, and we *do* need to go to school."

And she'd show him, for the millionth time, the scrap of newspaper with the picture of the split-faced children on it. The picture showed the same two children twice, once with their

24

split faces, and once with their split faces
somehow magically mended. They grinned
into the camera – proof, Gentle said, that there
really was a place where children with faces like
hers could be mended, made just like other
children. A special hospital perhaps, with very

clever doctors; she called it "Happy Split-face Land", and to Gentle it was a real place that – one day – she would go to, and be mended like the children in her picture.

Chipo suspected that the printed words around the picture might prove that there was no such place, or it was so far away that it was impossible to get to; but as neither he nor his sister could read, *this* just proved the other part of Gentle's argument: that they should both go to school and learn to read.

So there was nothing to be done about it. He didn't really mind. It kept Gentle happy and left him free to be the man of the family and make proper, important plans. So he told her, "Well done, little sis! Five hundred bags in one day! You must be hungry, eh?"

Gentle nodded. She sat back and watched Chipo pull the sandwich out from his sack, like a conjurer doing an especially good trick.

"Sandwiches," he told her. "And in a special-shaped box."

Solemnly Gentle took the triangular box from Chipo.

"We can have one each," he told her, but Gentle shook her head.

"Half now. Half in the morning."

Chipo's stomach hurt, he was so hungry. He wanted to take a whole sandwich and jam it into his mouth all at once. But he knew Gentle was right. She was sensible about some things. So he watched quietly as she put one sandwich into the broken plastic box they called "the larder" and laid the other on their one small chipped plate, and then placed this carefully on the upturned crate they called "the table". She broke the sandwich into two pieces and gave the biggest one to Chipo.

"Eat it *slow*," she told him. "Make it last!"

Chipo grinned at her and finished it in two bites. "No time for slow eating tonight!" he said, licking his fingers. "Superhero Chipo has a special mission!"

Gentle rolled her eyes. Chipo ignored his little sister's lack of respect and went on, "I found a TV today at the Old Dump. I hid it and marked the place so I can go back and get it tonight. I can trade it for a tin roof to keep us dry in the rainy season."

Gentle was not impressed, not at all. "Have you gone crazy?" she said. "If Papa Fudu finds out you took something from his dump, you'll be in big trouble."

"He won't find out." Chipo shrugged as if he wasn't concerned at all. "Anyway, you think he got his big house by obeying the rules?" He stood up and slung his bag over his shoulder.

But Gentle wasn't finished.

"How will you get through the fence?"

"Hey . . . this is Chipo you're talking to," he swaggered. "I know where there is a hole!"

"And what about the guards and the guard dogs?"

"Oh, those – that's just a story to scare people. There's no guards at the Old Dump and the dogs all died years ago!" Chipo grinned his most confident grin. "It'll be fine. And we'll have a roof in time for the rainy season."

Gentle leaped to her feet and pulled him back towards her. "If you are going, I'm coming with you," she said. Her chin stuck out and her eyes blazed.

"OK, OK," Chipo said. When Gentle got that cross there was no point trying to argue with her. He sighed. His sister was really nothing like her name.

Chapter 4

It was a very dark night with no moon and just a few stars showing between the clouds. This was good in one way, because it hid them, but bad in another because it made finding a way through the fence very hard. They had paced back and forth along a stretch of fence where Chipo *knew* the hole was, without finding it. He was just about to give up when Gentle said, "It's here."

"Where?" he said crossly.

"Give me your hand and I'll show you."

Gentle guided Chipo's hand to the place where the links in the mesh of wire had come loose and were held together by just one looped strand. With a bit of pulling and wiggling there was quite a good hole, easily big enough to allow two small, skinny bodies to climb up and inch their way through.

In a moment they were on the other side of the fence and Chipo had forgotten his bad temper. His eyes were completely accustomed to the darkness now; he could make out the pale surface of the dump, and the dark shapes of trees and bushes against it and against the sky. He'd find that TV in no time.

"All we have to do is walk in a straight line from here," he explained to Gentle. "When we get to the bushes, we turn right, up a slope, and we should see the bag marking the place."

Gentle wasn't listening. "How will we find the hole again?" she said.

Chipo hadn't thought of that. "I know where the hole is – just beyond the fifteenth fence post from the gate."

"Then how come you couldn't find it?"

Chipo didn't reply.

"I'll tie my face bandage to the wire right here," Gentle went on. "It's white – it'll stand out, and I don't need to wear it on the dump."

Chipo wished he'd thought of that. He was the big brother, and big brothers were supposed to be the ones with ideas, not little sisters. "Come on," he told Gentle. "Follow me."

Even without seeing her, Chipo knew that Gentle was rolling her eyes.

They walked out into the open space of the dump. Away from the fence they were less likely to be spotted, but more likely to get lost.

Chipo pushed his worry down into his belly, away from his heart, and walked on.

"Don't be scared," he told Gentle.

"I'm not scared," she replied, but he could tell she was.

There was a little more starlight now, so the surface of the dump looked like a big pale desert and Gentle's eyes glinted in her face. All Chipo could hear was the *shush-shush* of their feet on the crunchy top layer of the rubbish. Yet Gentle was sure she had heard something else. She made Chipo stop and listen.

"I heard footsteps," she said. "I know I did, Chipo!"

Gentle sounded scared, and Chipo couldn't help being pleased. In future she'd understand that Special Missions weren't meant for little sisters. "There's no one here but us!" he told her.

"Then why are you whispering?"

"I'm not whispering!" whispered Chipo.
"Now let's *go*!"

Chipo's carrier-bag flag worked well, and they soon found the spot where the TV was buried. He told Gentle to keep watch while he dug it out. He didn't think there was anything to watch out for, but it would keep her quiet. He slid his hands down through the bits and bobs and fragments of long-forgotten objects, dry and crumbly as ashes, until his fingers found the cool, smooth screen beneath. It wasn't broken, not even cracked; it still had its plastic casing, even all its little knobs and dials – Chipo could feel them all. He reached his arms right down around it and pulled.

"Chipo!"

Gentle's exclamation made Chipo let go of the TV and fall flat on his back with a scrunch.

"Chipo, I saw eyes. I did. It's the guard dogs coming to get us."

Chipo sat up, and was just about to get quite cross and tell Gentle to stop being a baby when he saw the green glint of a pair of slanted eyes in the darkness. The eyes stared, blinked, then moved. There was a rapid *shush-shush-shush-shush* of the animal's paws on the trash, then the eyes stared again. Could the stories about Fudu's guard dogs really be true? Chipo's heart was racing, but he answered Gentle calmly, as if a fierce killer guard dog was no more than a fly you swatted with your finger.

"Oh, *those* eyes. They're nothing to be scared of. If they come closer, throw a stick at 'em. Now let me get this TV."

Chipo plunged his arms back into the rubbish and found the solid square shape of the television again . . .

"Chipo," said Gentle, "the eyes are getting closer . . ."

Chipo didn't listen to his sister. Guard dog or no guard dog, he was going to get this TV! But it was stuck for some reason. He felt all around it . . .

"They're getting closer . . ." There was a whimper in Gentle's voice now, but Chipo took no notice – he was too busy pulling, and pulling, and—

"Oh, Chipo!" The fear in Gentle's voice changed, quite suddenly, to a giggle, and just as it did so, the TV came free of the dump, like a cork out of a bottle. Chipo, with the TV in his arms, somersaulted backwards, bowled Gentle off her feet and came to rest in a tangle of arms, legs and furry paws. When the two children opened their eyes, a dog was staring into their faces. It was hard to make out in the weak starlight, but the dog was huge, with a big square head, and paws bigger than the palms of Gentle's hands. But it wasn't fierce at all. Its skinny tail wagged back and forth against the sky, and its right ear – the left was just a stump – cocked in a friendly sort of way. It stood right over Gentle and looked down at her.

"Uff!" said the dog softly. "Uu-uff?" Its voice was deep and gruff.

"It wants to be my friend!" laughed Gentle.

"It wants to be fed!" said Chipo. "Or it wants to bark and give us away! Shoo! Shoo!" He waved his arms at the dog, then threw the slat that had held up the carrier-bag flag at it, and it fled into the darkness, its tail between its legs.

Gentle sat up and slapped Chipo hard on the back.

"Ow!" he exclaimed. "That really hurt!"

"Why did you chase it away?" Gentle complained.

"Do you want to share our food with

a *dog*?" Chipo replied crossly.

"But it wanted to be my *friend*," Gentle almost wailed.

Suddenly Chipo understood. Nobody wanted to be Gentle's friend. *He* was the only friend she had, and that didn't count because he hadn't chosen her, he was just her brother.

"I'm sorry," he said. "If it comes back I'll be nice to it. It can come home with us and eat my half-sandwich."

Gentle sniffed. "Thanks, Chipo," she said. "Shall I help carry the TV?"

"Yeah, that would be good," said Chipo, as calmly as he could; it was important, if you were a superhero like Powerbolt, to keep your head and be kind, even if you were really scared. He wondered if Gentle had noticed how very far they were from the hole in the fence, and safety.

Chapter 5

The TV was heavy and awkward to carry, and the children had to keep pausing to rest or get a better grip. Each time they stopped, Gentle looked out for her dog, calling out to it in whispers, but there was no sign of it. Chipo told Gentle that he thought he could hear its footsteps, but really he was just saying that to keep her happy.

As they walked and stopped, walked and stopped, Chipo made plans for the TV. He'd have to get it to the other end of Rubbish

Town; he couldn't trade it under Papa Fudu's nose! But once he was out of Fudu's usual patch there would be no stopping him. The TV was much more splendid than he could ever have hoped. He could trade it for enough tin to make walls for the crater as well as a roof. Blankets too, maybe, and food – dried beans and rice and a stove.

A stove! Something flashed across Chipo's mind: a wood stove, and rain beating on the roof, and a woman's voice singing. He tried to hold onto this memory, to see it more clearly, but it was gone as soon as it had come, quicker than a raindrop on dry sand.

They'd reached the fence, and there was Gentle's face bandage, marking their escape route. She untied the bandage and they got ready to lift the TV through the wire. Chipo was anxious: this was the most dangerous part of the operation. If they were caught now, there could be no doubt that they were stealing from Papa Fudu.

"Look!" Gentle cried. "There!"

Chipo gave a start; then he realized that she was looking out for the dog. He peered into the dark, and green eyes shone back at him! But something had scared the dog again. It turned and ran, and a moment later Chipo and Gentle found out why. The darkness was shattered with blinding light and shouting voices; somebody had been hiding in the bushes beside the fence. They had been caught.

"Put the TV down!" ordered a boy's voice from behind the torches.

Chipo held his arm up to shade his eyes, trying to see how many they were and what they were armed with – sticks or something worse. But the glare was too bright. He pulled

Gentle behind him to shield her while she put on her bandage.

"No good covering it up, girl," said a second voice. "We've seen what a freak you are."

Chipo knew that voice: Owiti! His heart fell to his feet. He would lose his job with Papa Fudu, and even if Fudu didn't beat him, now that Owiti knew about Gentle they'd never have any peace.

"Well," Owiti said. "How pleased Papa Fudu will be to hear his little favourite is stealing from him. I expect he'll give you to my brothers to deal with. Then who'll watch over your split-faced sister?"

Chipo was trying to think fast. But it was difficult with all this light flooding his eyes, and Owiti's malice and his own anger stopping his ears. He felt Gentle's hand slip into his. She'd finished bandaging her face and came to stand beside him. She was so little. He had to protect her. *Think quick, move fast; think quick, move fast*.

"Our big brother – that's who'll protect her!" Chipo shouted. "That's who'll come to get you, Owiti, if you lay a finger on her or me."

"Yeah, your big brother, who I've never seen. Who nobody's ever seen." Owiti was jeering, but Chipo could hear a seed of doubt in his voice.

"Well, if that's a risk you want to take . . ." Chipo kept his voice strong and sneering, when inside his heart was doing a horrible little dance.

"Don't talk," Owiti snarled. "You always talk and talk. But I know where you live now – in a little rat hole, with your witch sister. We've been there! Haven't we, boys?"

There was a chorus of laughs and yeses.

Owiti swaggered closer and his gang followed. Now Chipo could see them beyond the brightness of the torches. Four boys, all about Owiti's age – thirteen or fourteen – all big and bony and mean. They carried big sticks. They might do anything.

Owiti bent down, thrusting his face close to the torch so that light shone on his horse teeth and fat cheeks. "We ate that sandwich," he boasted. "We smashed your plate and we took this!"

Owiti was holding Gentle's tin of pennies and treasures. He pulled out the little doll and crushed it to dust in his hand; then he took her mother's blue bead and threw it far into the dump. Finally he tipped Gentle's hard-earned money straight into his pockets. Through their joined hands Chipo felt Gentle begin to tremble. Owiti thought this was the best joke in the world.

"Shaking with fear now, little freak?" he laughed. "Good!"

But Chipo could tell it was anger, not fear, that was making Gentle shake. Suddenly she let go of his hand and stepped right up to Owiti. She pushed the bandage off her face in a single movement, and began to speak in a low, stern voice.

Owiti moved back, and tried to mock her voice, but when he heard what she was saying he fell silent.

"You're right," she said. "I *am* a witch . . ."

Chipo stared at his sister, wondering if she'd gone completely mad.

Gentle spoke some more. In the dancing black shadows of the torchlight, the voice that came out of the split in her face was like a wicked spell.

"I have a spirit dog," the voice said, "with eyes like leaves and teeth that will rip out your souls . . ."

Chipo felt a shiver go down his back. Now Owiti and his gang looked truly frightened. Gentle wasn't mad after all – she'd just done some very quick thinking. Chipo was torn between being proud of her, and jealous that he never seemed to have such clever ideas.

He stood quietly beside her, trying to look as much like a witch's older brother as he could manage.

"If you don't believe me," Gentle went on in the deep witchy voice, "just look out there!" She raised her arm slowly and pointed into the blackness at the edge of the torchlight.

As if she had trained it for weeks, the dog moved into the light. Its head was down and its scrappy fur was on end. Its big body cast a huge shadow and its eyes blazed green. It growled like the earth moving, bared its teeth and began to walk towards Owiti and the other boys.

Owiti's gang backed away in confusion, their torch beams shooting off in all directions.

"Run!" Chipo breathed to his sister, and they ran, away from the fence and the searching lights, into the dark cover of the Old Dump.

Chapter 6

Running over the dump was like running over sand: their feet sank and slipped, making it hard to move fast. The boys' torches had blinded them too, so they couldn't see where they were going. Gentle's short legs were tiring already, and she slowed and stopped.

"Oh," she gasped, "I wish I *was* a witch, then we could fly instead of running."

"I'd believe you were a witch after that," Chipo said, "but we've got to keep moving or they'll catch us."

"But where can we go?" Gentle panted.

"Just away from Owiti, for now," Chipo gasped back.

"I will put a spell on him!" said Gentle in her witch's voice.

In spite of his beating heart, Chipo almost smiled. "Never mind spells," he told her. "Just run, little witch!"

The shouts and yells of Owiti's gang were fading behind them. Gentle's witch act was enough to hold them back for a while, but sooner or later they would gather their courage and follow. So, Chipo thought, he and Gentle must make the most of their advantage now. If they could keep out of range of the boys' torches, they might have a chance — at least until the sun came up. After that, he didn't want to think.

Gentle put her hand on his arm. "Wait!" she said.

"We can't wait; if we wait they'll catch us."

"Look! There's the dog. It wants us to follow."

Gentle was right. There *was* the dog, trotting up ahead, its pale body just visible like a little ghost running over the dump. Chipo had to admit that it was pretty weird how the dog kept looking round at them, and was definitely not going at top speed. It even seemed to stop sometimes to let them catch up.

So they followed the dog because, Chipo chided himself, he didn't have a better idea. All he knew was that they had lost everything: their home in the bomb crater, his job with Fudu, Gentle's precious savings, and her bead and doll. They couldn't go back to Rubbish Town now.

They seemed to run for hours. The sound of their pursuers' voices fell further and further behind, but the eastern sky was growing light;

Chipo knew that if they had nowhere to hide by daybreak, Owiti – or even Papa Fudu himself – would come to find them. He wondered how it would be to just cover themselves with rubbish and lie still all day. Hot – that's how it would be, he concluded; way too hot.

"Come on, Chipo!" Gentle hissed over her

shoulder. "The dog – she's got a place for us to hide!"

Chipo looked ahead: a line of darkness showed where bushes grew on the slope of a trash mountain. The dog's pale shape looked back once, then disappeared, and the children followed.

Under the gnarled roots of some bushes the dog had dug out a little cave. Its sides were squashed rubbish and its roof was the dense canopy of branches and leaves. Chipo followed Gentle, wriggling under a dipping root, into a space only just a little smaller than the bottom of their very own crater. The floor was littered with well-chewed rat bones and thoroughly licked tins, and a trickle of smelly liquid ran along the left-hand side: doggy food and doggy water.

It wasn't that much stinkier than the rest of the dump, Chipo thought, and it did feel pretty safe. He and Gentle sat with their backs against the dry back wall of the dog's den. They could just make out the dog, wagging its tail in the gloom. It came up to Gentle, licked her hand and then dropped something into her lap – probably a rat bone for welcome, Chipo thought, and wondered if Gentle would now have to chew it to be polite; but Gentle gasped in a way that said the dog's gift definitely *wasn't* an old bone.

"It's Mama's bead!" she exclaimed. "The dog found it!"

Gentle flung her arms around the dog's neck, and for a minute the two of them were just one big shape in the darkness.

"I've got some string in my bag," Chipo said. "If you give me the bead I'll put it on the string for you and you can keep it round your neck."

"Thanks, Chipo!" Gentle passed the cool bead into his hand. It was as big as the end of a man's thumb, but still pretty small to have been found in the featureless dump. He held it for a moment and wished *he* could have found his sister's precious bead for her; he wished *he* could have come up with the plan that had saved them from Owiti; and most of all he wished he'd never found that wretched TV.

The dog and Gentle soon fell asleep, curled up together like puppies, but Chipo waited, watchful and alert for the sound of voices and the flash of torches. They never came, and as the grey dawn light sifted into their lair, he risked a peek out through the greenery to see if he could work out where in the dump they were. But there were no familiar landmarks, and the trash hills all around were too high to see very far. They were in a part of the Old Dump where he'd never been, so perhaps they'd be safe from Papa Fudu's gangs of workers, at least for a day. He lay down with his back to Gentle and the dog, and went to sleep.

Chapter 7

When Chipo woke, he felt like a wet rag. The fine dreams of the future that he'd had such a short time ago were all gone. They couldn't go back to their crater home; they couldn't go back to their jobs; Gentle had lost her money; and all they had left was his canvas bag containing a plastic water bottle and a broken knife. It wasn't much to build on. He lay still and felt his heart sink in his chest like a stone. He'd never be able to think quick or move fast ever again.

He looked around. Now he'd got used to the

smell, he realized that the dog's home was a very good place to hide. Sunlight came through the layers of dense leaves above, bathing the den in a cool green glow. The dog – which was a female, as Gentle had thought – was chasing fleas over her backside with smartly clicking front teeth, and Gentle was sitting beside her drawing something on her bandage with a broken biro that Chipo had found for her on the dump. They looked as comfortable and familiar as a family sitting round a fire.

Chipo felt lonely and he wriggled over to join them. The dog greeted him with a brief tail-wag, then went back to flea-catching, and Gentle gave him her best split-face smile. Gentle could be fierce but she never seemed to blame him when things went wrong, which made him feel just a little better.

He offered her water from the bottle in his

bag. She took a small sip and returned to her drawing. Chipo waited for her to ask him what they were going to do, hoping that when she asked, an answer would come to him.

But Gentle didn't ask; instead she said, "I'm making a map."

Chipo didn't want to admit that he wasn't sure what a map was. But whatever it was, while Gentle was making it she might not ask difficult questions about what they were going to do next, so he asked, "How will we make a map?"

"Well," Gentle said, her face creasing up with the effort of thinking, "a real map is made of paper, with pictures on. I don't have any paper so I thought I could use the bandage."

Chipo didn't feel he understood the idea of maps any better after this, so he leaned over Gentle's drawing and took a closer look.

"A map," she continued, "is meant to show

where you've been and where you are going, so you can find your way."

She pointed to the left-hand side of the bandage: she had drawn a round hut with a roof and a little chimney poking through. Beside the hut were seven figures in a line from tall to small.

"This is a picture of where we used to live. That's Mama, that's Papa, then there's Azi and Daren, our big brothers, and Patience, our sister; then there's us."

Chipo stared at the line of stick people, all the same except for size. That must be him, next to the end, between Patience and Gentle, who must have been the littlest.

"Here's the planes and the bombs," Gentle went on quietly, "and here's everybody all dead, and here's you and me, running away, alive."

She had told Chipo this story before, always

in the same way, without getting sad, and always making it sound like a triumph that the two of them had escaped with their lives. He tried and tried to remember it for himself, but whenever he searched his mind he found nothing. Gentle told him that it was a good thing he didn't remember; that sometimes she would rather not remember the day when bombs had fallen on their village and taken away their family. But it was the time *before* the bombs that Chipo wished and wished he could remember.

Gentle's next pictures showed people chasing the two children away from groups of huts that were meant to be villages. There were snatches of that time that he remembered, but his real memory of their past only began with Rubbish Town and the dump.

Gentle had drawn their little home in the

crater, along with their plate and their table. And she'd drawn the fence round the Old Dump, the TV, and two stick people and a dog running away from some other stick people, who were Owiti and his gang.

"I'm sorry about the TV," Chipo said sadly. "We've lost our home because of me and that TV."

"It doesn't matter, Chipo," said Gentle. "That's just another part of where we've been. What matters is where we're *going*!"

She wound her way right to the other end of the bandage, where she had carefully pinned the picture from the magazine of the children with split faces like hers. Around it she had drawn pictures of trees and flowers; she'd even added a large dog with its tail in the air.

"Happy Split-face Land!" said Gentle, pointing. "That's where we're going, so I can be mended and we can go to school."

"But it's not a *real* place, Gentle," said Chipo crossly. "We can't go to a place that isn't real."

"It is a real place, it *is*!" she said, crossing her arms on her chest and sticking out her chin. "We just need to find out how to get there. That's what this map is for: to show where we've been and where we're going so we can find the way!"

Chipo's mouth fell open and stayed that way. He didn't have an answer. To cover his confusion he poked his finger at the middle of Gentle's map where no pictures had been drawn.

"Look," he said, "there's nothing but blank bandage between where we've been and where we're going. So how does that help us find the way?"

"That's your job, Chipo-Powerbolt-*Superhero*.

Think quick, move fast!" Gentle snapped her fingers under his nose and rolled up her bandage-map.

Chipo sat quietly and took some deep breaths; his sister was completely, *completely* maddening. Now he was going to have to find the way to a place that didn't exist!

He sighed, and then he smiled. Well, at least he didn't feel like a wet rag with a stone for a heart any more! Finding the way to an imaginary place was definitely a job for a Chipo who could think quick and move fast!

Every journey, even one to a place that you don't believe is real, has to have a first step. But all the first steps that Chipo thought of seemed to lead straight to dead ends: they could wait until dark, then go back to the hole in the fence – but Owiti would have closed it up or, worse still, might be waiting for them there; they could look for another hole to let them out of the dump – but with no food and only a small amount of water, they could die searching the miles and miles of fence. Rats and the stinky green water were OK for a dog, but if humans tried it, they'd get sick.

All morning, while the den under the bushes grew hotter and hotter and stinkier and stinkier, Chipo went between these two first steps in his head, like a dog pacing back and forth between two bare bones.

Gentle had decided to call the dog Mouse, even though Chipo had never seen an animal less like a mouse in all his life. Mouse lay with her head in Gentle's lap having her ears stroked, and if dogs can smile, she was smiling. Chipo wondered if Gentle would give up on her dream of Happy Split-face Land if she could stay here for ever with her new friend.

Maybe Gentle could live on stinky water and raw rats.

Just when he was pacing between his two ideas for about the millionth time, the ground began to shake. Bits of old tin and crumbling plastic fell out of the walls of the den. Mouse jumped to her feet, her thin tail pressed between her legs. She began to snarl and then to whimper, but soon her voice was drowned out by a huge roaring sound. Gentle clung to Mouse, and Chipo held tight to Gentle. But, as the den collapsed and the bushes were torn from their roots, Chipo's arms were pulled away from Gentle and he felt himself being rolled over and over in a smelly, suffocating tidal wave of trash.

The roaring and rolling went on and on and on. Rubbish filled Chipo's eyes and ears and nose. He felt it fighting to get into his mouth and down into his lungs and belly. It seemed to want to fill him up altogether. He fought for every breath and tried to move and struggle free, but with every roar and every roll he was pressed down harder, held more tightly by the dense bundle of bits and pieces.

At last the roaring lessened and the world no longer shook. But Chipo couldn't move: he was buried alive, squashed inside rubbish packed so tight he couldn't even open his eyes. He listened for clues as to what had happened . . . there was a rumbling sound beneath him. He was on a truck, being bumped up and down inside his trash cocoon as it moved over the dump and then out onto the rutted road. They were escaping from the dump – he tried to call out to tell Gentle the good news, but he had no voice, no breath, and soon nothing in his head but darkness.

Chapter 8

Chipo dreamed of water running over his tongue and down his throat. He dreamed that his body was dried up and dead, like an old date, and that the water pumped him up, smooth and alive again.

And then he woke up. His tongue was thick and swollen, and his eyes felt as if they were full of stones. It was hard to think, but he knew that thinking was really important and that he must keep trying to do it.

There was no rumbling or bumping any

more. The rubbish in which he was bound and crushed was moving smoothly now, with the slightest tremor and hum. The sound was nice, soothing, and disturbed only a little by a sound of metal hinges creaking and doors slamming shut every minute or so. Chipo felt as if he would just like to lie still and listen to the hum and clanking for ever.

"Uff? . . . Uu-uff!" a tiny, faint voice was calling to him from somewhere. "Uff! Uff! *Uff!*" it said.

"Mouse?" Chipo's brain suggested, and then, "Gentle?" The hot dry fog that had clogged his mind lifted in an instant. Gentle and Mouse were trapped like he was, and it was his job to get them out, right now!

He began to wriggle and squirm. Tiny movements at first, but as he pushed back at the rubbish that held him, it yielded a little

and gradually began to let him go; first his
fingertips could move, then his whole hand;
then he could shrug one shoulder, and bend
a bit at the elbow. He spat the stuff out of
his mouth, coughed it out of his lungs, and
struggled with all the strength he could muster.
Something familiar touched his fingers: it was
the strap of his bag, caught beside him in the
crush. Chipo inched the rough woven string
into his grasp and pulled, pulled, pulled, little
by little by little. At last he could feel the lip
of the bag, then its side, and then . . . then . . .
then . . . inside, the lovely smooth coolness of
the broken knife. He got it into his hand and
began to saw away gently – just enough to take
the smallest slices from the daintiest of cakes;
then he made slashes, good enough to skin
a rabbit. He cleared enough space to get one
arm above his head, and sliced a path forward,

cutting with his knife and pushing with his stiff, cramped feet.

Just like a worm edging its way through the earth, Chipo squirmed his way out of the giant heap of rubbish in which he had been imprisoned, and poked his head out. The air was hot and not very fresh, but it was still wonderful to be able to breathe properly. He lay there with just his head sticking out, exhausted. He remembered the water bottle in his bag – there was just a mouthful left, but it revived him.

He looked around and saw that he was inside a huge metal building, ten, twenty, a hundred times bigger than anything in Rubbish Town. Electric lights blazed in the roof and, in every direction, thousands of huge round bales of crushed rubbish were stacked on a slowly moving conveyor belt. At the very

end of the building were metal doors, which
Chipo could see and hear opening to let the
bales into the fiery furnace that burned on the
other side. Everyone in Rubbish Town had
always suspected that Fudu had bigger plans
for the Old Dump than collecting plastic
bottles and scrap metal, and this was it: he was
scooping up all the old rubbish and burning it;
and if someone had built a swanky warehouse
like this, somehow this burning
must be worth a lot of money.

Fear shot through Chipo
like lightning, straightening his
wobbly legs and strengthening
his sore arms. Inside one of
those bales was his sister, and
he had to find her before the
clanking door opened and
burned her to a crisp.

Chapter 9

Chipo struggled out of his bale and jumped down onto the conveyor belt. It was moving quite slowly, and the bale he'd been in was a long way from the doors. So there was no need to panic yet, he told himself; there was time to find Gentle.

He still felt like a dried-up date and his tongue stuck to the roof of his mouth, so when he called out, his voice was small and cracked. "Gentle? Mouse? Where are you?"

The only sound to come back to him was

the faint crackling of the electric lights, the hum of the conveyor, and another loud creak and clang from the furnace doors.

He'd have to check every bale, starting with the ones close to the furnace. No good finding that Gentle wasn't in the bales far from the fire if she was already too close to those doors to be saved. Chipo ran down the conveyor belt, slapping every bale and calling again and again. Some of the ones he'd checked were already near the furnace doors. What if he'd somehow missed Gentle – if she was too weak to call out? Chipo felt another terrible wave of fear. He leaned against the nearest bale for support, and a strange little black object caught his attention. He looked more closely and saw that it was a dog's nose! He put his cheek to the rubbery nostrils and felt the faintest trace of breath. Maybe Mouse and Gentle were still together.

In moments Chipo had pulled Mouse free, and she was standing beside him coughing and sneezing, her legs as wobbly as his had been.

Chipo reached inside the hole he'd pulled Mouse out of, calling Gentle's name and burrowing frantically, trying to find her. Mouse was no help at all: she barked and then worried at his leg with her teeth. When Chipo ignored her, she started to bite him very hard, and when he whirled round to push her off, she let go, and dashed down the line of bales towards the furnace doors, barking loudly and looking back at him.

At last Chipo understood, and ran after her.

Three bales back from the clanking furnace doors she stopped, put her paws up on the side of a bale and worried something free with her teeth: the end of a stained white bandage, smudged with drawings.

"Good dog, Mouse!" Chipo cried.

"Uff-uff!" said Mouse, and began to scrabble and bite at the tightly packed rubbish with her teeth and paws.

They were nearly out of time. The conveyor belt was inching unstoppably forward. In just a few moments the bale with Gentle inside would move through the clanking doors and be swallowed by fire. There wasn't time to burrow slowly through to where Gentle was caught or to find what controlled the conveyor belt and switch it off; there wasn't time to lever the heavy bale off the conveyor, even if Chipo had had the strength or the tools to do it. All he could do was to slash at the cords that held the rubbish scrunched together, and hope that the bale would fall apart and let his sister free.

Like a spider, Chipo ran up the side of the bale, digging in his fingers and toes so he could scramble higher. He drew out his broken half-knife and began to cut and saw at the first cord, across the middle of the bale. It gave way with a dull *pop*, and the bale sagged outwards like a fat person growing suddenly tired of pulling in their tummy.

The belt moved on. The bale just in front of Gentle's stood at the doors, and Chipo felt a blast of heat as they opened to take it in; he heard the big *wumphh* as the whole thing burst into flames. Down at the bottom of the bale, Mouse began to whimper.

Chipo started on the next cord, but it was tougher than the first. He threw all his weight and strength into pulling the knife back and forth, back and forth, over the tight cord. But the knife simply couldn't manage the last strand. In frustration Chipo yanked at it with both hands; it broke with a snap, and the rubbish flowed out very suddenly, knocking him off balance and sending him falling out and down, away from the bale. He clutched at the dangling end of the cord, and caught it in one hand. But the fatly sagging bale was now off balance, and Chipo dangling on the end of the cord was all it needed to make it give up the struggle to stay upright. Just as the conveyor belt made its final glide forward towards the opening doors, the bale toppled sideways. It fell down on top of Chipo as he hit the floor, pulling the barking Mouse with it, and burst open like a huge egg.

Bruised and dazed, and once more spitting rubbish out of his mouth, Chipo stood up. There in the middle of the burst bale lay Gentle, clutching the end of her bandage with one hand and patting Mouse with the other.

"You found me, Chipo Superhero!" she breathed.

Chipo was so happy to see her that his chest hurt and he couldn't speak. So it was perhaps a good thing that there wasn't time for talking. Something about the falling bale had set off flashing red lights and loud blaring alarms. They could hear men shouting, and feet pounding along in hard boots. Guards! Chipo was sure that whoever owned this shiny new factory wouldn't like two kids and a dog from the dump messing things up. Gentle was too weak to run so he pulled her onto his back and snapped his fingers to call Mouse close.

"Come on," he said. "We've got to hide!"

At first it seemed as if there was nowhere to hide in this place. It was just a giant metal box, with the conveyor belt snaking and winding its way over the floor, and up to the doors to the furnace. But in spite of the sirens and the flashing lights, nothing seemed to stop the march of the belt taking rubbish bales to be burned. So by keeping the moving bales between themselves and the approaching guards, Chipo, Gentle and Mouse could move and hide at the same time. Chipo guessed that if the guards never actually caught sight of them, they would assume that the bale had fallen off all by itself, and they would be left to escape in peace.

He peeked out from behind a bale: the guards had big boots and smart blue overalls, but none of them looked very grown up. They clustered around the burst bale looking puzzled.

Dodging round one bale after another, Chipo, Gentle and Mouse were soon quite a distance away from the guards, at the entrance to the warehouse. Here the bales of rubbish on their conveyor came in through a flapping curtain of plastic strips. Hot, swampy-smelling night air blew in as each bale pushed through on the conveyor, but it was impossible to see what lay beyond the curtain. Shouts and tramping boots were coming close again now, as the guards decided to search a bit harder for whatever had caused the problem. There was only one thing to do: Chipo held Gentle tight and, with Mouse beside him, ran through the curtain to find that there was no floor beyond it, and that the three of them were falling through the muggy night air.

Chapter 10

They landed in deep water. Mouse was the only one who really knew how to swim; Chipo and Gentle just improvised, which was particularly hard for Gentle. She coughed and spluttered and splashed but, like Chipo, somehow managed to avoid drowning. Luckily the water was soon shallow enough for wading.

Patches of light glinted darkly on the still surface, but it was too dim to see properly. Chipo was glad, because the water smelled horrible and had things floating in it that he really didn't want to see. He hoped they were nothing worse than dead rats. Even though he was as thirsty as a desert, he was thankful that none of the water had passed his lips.

There was no sign that the guards had followed them out of the warehouse, so for now they were safe; all the same Chipo thought it best to stay out of sight, so they waded under the warehouse, which stood on tall pillars over the swamp, and then out the other side. Gentle had recovered a little but she was still shaky, and she held onto Chipo's arm without a word. He wondered if she knew how close she had come to being fried? He decided that he wouldn't tell her.

They splashed their way to what looked like the shore, a line of lumpy darkness that might have been trees or bushes or maybe just piles of trash. As the water grew ever shallower, and

Gentle and Mouse could both walk easily, Chipo turned to take a look at the building they'd escaped from.

The warehouse, now a kilometre or so behind them, was even bigger than it had seemed from the inside. Leading from it in all directions, like the threads of a huge spider's web, were cables that sparked with flashes of blue electricity. They glittered on the water and lit up a whole sea of rubbish bales standing outside, waiting to be loaded onto the conveyor, which led up the side of the building to the opening with the plastic strips.

"What is that place?" Gentle asked in a small voice.

"I think," said Chipo cautiously, "it's like a big generator making electricity from rubbish, like Fudu's generator makes it from petrol. I think Fudu is turning his dump into electricity!"

"What for? There aren't any houses or people here," Gentle said, shaking her head.

Chipo shrugged. "Maybe the electricity goes somewhere else, in those big cables."

He gazed at the blue-sparking cables, held up by spindly pylons, one after another. There were lines of them disappearing off into the darkness. Chipo guessed those pylons and cables went a long, long way, so the electricity in them was going somewhere – somewhere important. In a place important enough to need so much electricity, surely there would be opportunities for a quick-thinking, fast-moving person! Chipo began to feel much better as his mind filled with plans for following the sparking cables to wherever they were going.

Mouse interrupted his thoughts by whining and then being very sick.

"Oh no, she must have swallowed some of

that water," said Gentle. "I think I did too. Oh, Chipo, I feel sick." And with that she fell face down on the muddy shore.

Chipo turned her over and wiped her face with the bottom of his wet T-shirt. It was too dark to see her properly, but he could feel at once that this was something more serious than Gentle being tired or hungry or thirsty. She was breathing very fast, and her skin was ice-cold. Mouse licked her hand, and then turned aside to be violently sick again.

Gentle began to shiver, but she didn't wake up, even when Chipo patted her cheek and pulled on her arm. Mouse started whimpering, and shivering just like Gentle.

Chipo looked around and saw that what he had taken for odd-shaped boulders lying everywhere were TVs. Small, large, medium-sized, poking out of the water and littering the shore, numerous as pebbles. But what use were TVs to him now? How could they help make Gentle better? He had truly felt like a hero when they got out of the warehouse, and the sight of the electricity pylons marching into the darkness had filled him with all sorts of new plans, but now he felt useless. He was alone in the dark with no idea how to help his sister or his dog.

"They drank the swamp water, didn't they?"

For a moment Chipo wasn't sure whether

it was his own voice, speaking the worry in his head.

Then the voice spoke again. "Well?" it demanded. "Didn't they?"

"Yes!" Chipo replied with his head in his hands. "I think they did."

"Oh, that's bad, that is," said the voice. "Very bad."

Chipo couldn't work out where the voice was coming from. It seemed to be all around him, speaking out of the darkness itself. He stood up, put his hands on his hips and said, as boldly as he could manage, "Who are you? Show yourself!"

"Huh," said the voice. "No need for that! Only trying to help."

And then a dark shape that Chipo had taken for a boulder moved, unfolded and stepped forward.

Although the voice was human, even childlike, the creature it belonged to moved more like an animal than a person. It moved on all four limbs, although the front ones were clearly arms with hands, and it had a big curved back like a tortoise. Had it been able to stand upright, it would have been as tall as a big grown-up.

"My name is Tortu," it said as it lumbered towards Gentle and Mouse. Chipo was afraid it would hurt them, but it touched each in turn gently with long, knobbly fingers.

"Hmm," Tortu said. "Dog'll be OK. Girl, maybe. I will help. Pick her up and follow." And without waiting for Chipo's opinion on the matter, the creature turned on its four limbs and began to head off along the shore, almost disappearing in amongst the shadows between the TVs.

Very gently, Chipo picked up his sister and set off after the moving shape that was Tortu. Mouse limped slowly along behind them, occasionally turning aside to be sick.

Tortu moved fast for such an awkward being, and Chipo found he had to concentrate hard to keep up and avoid the endless half-buried, wrecked TVs that covered the shore more and more thickly the further they went. At last, up ahead, he saw a hut – long and low, with yellow light showing in its four windows and spilling from a door that opened as they approached. A wonderful smell of food flooded out with the light, a smell so welcoming and delicious that it overcame Chipo's fear of Tortu and this strange place with its wrecked TVs. He remembered how very, very, *very* hungry he was.

"Come on, come on," Tortu called from inside. "Quick!"

Chapter 11

Inside, the hut was brightly lit with electric lights, and Chipo could see Tortu clearly for the first time. He was a man, though how old it was impossible to guess. His skin was covered in huge scaly warts, so that his little red-rimmed eyes stared out from a mask of horny patches. His back was humped and his whole body bent forward, so he could easily drop to walk on all fours. Now he stood upright, or as upright as he could, swinging his strong muscly arms about and giving orders to the thirty or so children who crowded around a big table in the middle of the hut.

"Make a space quick," he told them. His voice seemed to come from the whole surface of his body, rather than simply from his mouth, like heat glowing from every part of a fire; and, just like flames, the children flinched when it touched them. They scuttled around, clearing a space under Tortu's direction. More children peered out from the bunk beds that lined the far end of the hut. One particularly small child stood on a box to stir a huge pot of meat stew on a little round stove, above which were shelves piled with more tins and packets of food than Chipo had ever seen in his life before; not even Papa Fudu's kitchen was so well supplied.

"Here," Tortu told Chipo, pointing at the table. "Put her down here."

Chipo laid Gentle down, and silently the children gathered round, staring warily, first at Gentle and then at Chipo. Chipo found himself staring back just as warily, because he had never seen children like this before. They were well fed for sure; none had skinny legs or sticking-out ribs like him and Gentle, but their faces were covered in strange growths like dollops of mud made of skin, or were scaly like snakes; several had small humps on their backs like Tortu; many had eyes that were milky blue; most had no hair. All of them had coughs or wheezes, so that Chipo had the impression that he was in a room full of sickly lizards. He concluded that this must be a place where such unfortunate children could come to be cared for; perhaps this meant that Tortu really *was* trying to help, and that Gentle's Happy Split-face Land wasn't so crazy after all.

Tortu gave more orders: "Get me the salt water, the charcoal drink and the equipment."

Three children immediately rushed over to some shelves and cupboards, pulling out bottles, bowls and cups, a rubber tube and a funnel.

Tortu looked at Chipo, and might have been smiling under his scales. "I will help her. Do not be worried."

Chipo couldn't help it. Tortu and his gang of children were so strange, so monstrous, and Gentle looked so small, so very nearly not there at all. Chipo's heart was in his throat and he asked himself what sort of superhero brother let his sister swallow swamp water.

The children brought Tortu the long rubber tube with the big funnel on the end. Before Chipo had the chance to ask anything about it, Tortu slipped the tube down Gentle's throat,

and was pouring white liquid from a bottle
into the funnel at the other end.

"What are you doing?" Chipo grabbed at
the tube, but Tortu slapped his hand away so
hard it left his fingers numb.

"I told you," Tortu growled. "I will help her.
Hold him."

Several pairs of small, scaly hands grabbed
Chipo and held his arms tight.

Tortu pulled out the tube and called for a
bowl – just in time, as, almost at once, Gentle
began to retch.

"That's a good, good sign," Tortu said. "Being
sick will take the poison water from her belly."

That at least made sense; Chipo stopped
struggling and the children let him go. He held
Gentle's hand while Tortu put the tube down
her throat once more.

"This gets more poison out," he explained,

and poured a soot-black liquid into the
funnel. Chipo watched Gentle's face – her eyes
flickered open and closed again. He felt ready
to be sick with worry himself, but
Tortu said gruffly, "This girl
will live."

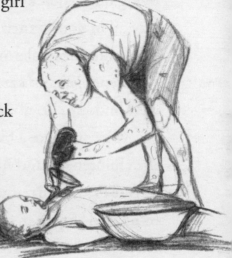

The children pressed
around the table,
chattering, but drew back
as Tortu told them off.

"Hush up and learn,"
he grumbled. "Salt
water first to
make 'em sick,
then charcoal
water to pull more poison out. Anyone
swallow swamp water," he continued sternly,
"you do this, or they'll die quick-quick!"

The children all fell silent and nodded

solemnly, but out of the darkness of one of the top bunks, a red-eyed, scaly-faced boy appeared and began to speak.

"Could be," his voice rasped, "could be that dying quick-quick is better than slow-slow, the way all of *us* is dying!"

A murmur of alarm passed through the children, like a breeze through leaves.

"Shuddup, Eric," Tortu snarled. "Shuddup!" His voice was like a blast from a furnace, and the children around him drew back.

But Eric wasn't afraid: he leaned out of the bunk and shook an arm, thin and scaly as a chameleon's, at Tortu. "They all know they're dying. Look at them! *Look at me!*" Eric's voice faded into a fit of coughs, but his words had taken root: some of the children had begun to cry.

Tortu stood up as straight as he could and

turned his back on Eric. "You won't listen to him!" he ordered the children. "You are not dyin'! You are alive, and this is a good place."

A few faint murmurs of agreement came from around the table.

"Yes? *Yes?*" Tortu shouted, and it was more like an order than a question. "You have food and you are safe. You don't need more than that. Now," he said, dropping back from a yell to a growl, "we eat."

Everyone began to rush around collecting bowls and spoons, and boxes and chairs to sit on around the long table. Eric was forgotten; only Chipo was watching him as he slowly turned and crawled back into the shadows, coughing.

"Put your girl in that bunk over there," Tortu told Chipo gruffly. "Then we all eat. Your dog too."

Mouse – still a little trembly after the swamp water – stood in the doorway, but she wouldn't come in until Tortu had stopped looking at her.

Chipo laid Gentle down on a bottom bunk towards the end of the hut. He put their mama's bead in her hand, and her bandage map on her chest. She wasn't clammy and cold any more, but she was deeply asleep. Mouse came and sat beside her and licked her hand.

"She's OK, Mouse," Chipo said. "She just needs to sleep." He stroked Mouse's ears and told her what a good dog she was, then went to eat, leaving Gentle in her care.

The strange children were crowding round the table, eating and chattering. Tortu sat at the head, watching with his small darting eyes. He pointed to Chipo's place at the far end of the table, away from the other children.

Perhaps they found Chipo as strange as he found them.

Chipo sat down and stared at them. It was so weird – as he looked around the table, he was reminded of his favourite *Powerbolt* episode, the one with the dinosaurs; if these children were bigger, he thought, they could easily be those scaly monsters. Yet they seemed pretty harmless, even if they weren't actually friendly. Although Tortu was clearly feared (Chipo could almost imagine him eating people like the monsters in *Powerbolt*), he *had* saved Gentle's life. And then there was Eric . . . It was all very confusing, and Chipo was very tired, and very hungry. He shook his head and turned his attention to the big bowl of meat stew in front of him; he hoped that if this *was* a peculiar dream, he wouldn't wake until he'd eaten it.

Chapter 12

Chipo ate until he was full, and no longer even a little bit hungry. Afterwards, he felt almost too tired to walk. As he dragged himself up into the bunk above Gentle's, he saw that she was sleeping with a smile at the corners of her mouth and Mouse flopped on her legs like a bag of yams.

Chipo slept and slept. He dreamed about TVs lying underwater; he was bringing them to the surface for a smiling Papa Fudu, who hooked them onto giant electric wires and then handed him bags of money and big pots of meat stew in exchange.

He swam up through another pool of sleep towards the sound of a voice saying, "Up! Up! Trucks here! Work time!" and opened his eyes. Tortu was at the door, shouting, while his gang of children jumped down from their bunks and rushed outside. In the bright daylight Chipo could see their strange growths of skin and hair in horrible detail. But without the shadows around them, the children no longer looked like monsters or dinosaurs to him; they were just kids.

Seeing that Chipo was awake, Tortu called to him, "Come. All hands are useful." He too seemed less frightening and sinister in daylight.

Chipo swung his legs over the side of the bunk and jumped down. Gentle was still asleep, with the smile now at the edges of her eyes, Mouse draped over her legs. He glanced about: the hut was homely and welcoming in the sunlight. It felt safe. There could be no harm in leaving Gentle for a while, and Mouse would guard her. It would, in any case, be days before she could move, and he should learn all he could about Tortu's camp in case it proved useful.

Outside, the first thing Chipo saw was the swamp into which they had fallen after escaping from the warehouse. It was even more disgusting than he could have imagined. There *were* dead rats floating in it; there were dead animals of all sorts – lizards, snakes, birds, even a maribou! Gentle and Mouse were very lucky indeed to be alive if the swamp water could kill a tough old maribou stork. Beyond the swamp stood the warehouse, like a fat spider in the centre of a web of cables and pylons; now, in daylight, Chipo could follow the lines of pylons even further into the distance, and he found his heart lifting a little with excitement at the thought of following them.

But Tortu was calling, urging everyone to hurry, so there was no more time for scheming. The children rushed towards a big truck parked on a track between two small hills. Beyond the hills was a huge fence and metal gates, all crackling with electricity. Dried bodies and skeletons of birds and animals dotted the sparking wire mesh, showing what would happen to any living thing that tried to leave that way. Chipo had looked at the fence for a while, wondering why Tortu needed such fierce protection, before he realized what the twin hills were made of: TVs. Even yesterday, mountains of TVs would have been very exciting to Chipo, but now he was only a little curious. Other people might want to work with old TVs, but now he had bigger dreams, full of sparking pylons.

Tortu was shouting instructions: "Yellow team unload; blue team load; red team form a line."

Chipo hadn't noticed before, but the children were colour-coded, dressed in different T-shirts. Those in yellow were the least scaly; they stood up straight and ran when Tortu called out to them. The blue team were almost as lively, but their features were lost in scales and bumps. The children in red T-shirts moved more slowly than the yellows or the blues; some were bent over like Tortu, and several had milky-blue, blind eyes. Tortu issued orders to each group, giving the hardest work to the yellows and the easiest to the reds.

"Yellow team unload; blue team load; red team form a line," he repeated.

The children scuttled to obey; they made Chipo think of ants, the way they rushed around. As fast as the yellows unloaded, the blues passed other crates into the back of the truck. There was hardly any talking, but the children didn't seem worried; in fact they looked quite cheerful – as far as you could tell under their scales and lumps. Only the driver of the truck looked uneasy. He was dressed from head to foot in yellow overalls and wore a mask from which his frightened eyes peeped out.

The crates coming off the truck were full of food: tins and packets and cartons – even more kinds than were already on the shelves in the hut. But the contents of the crates going into the truck were far more mystifying; they were broken bits of TVs – all the wires and little circuit boards that Chipo recognized from smashed TVs in Rubbish Town. Looking

round at the twin TV mounds, Chipo saw
that one was made of whole TVs, and the
other, which ended tumbling into the waters
of the swamp, was made of TVs whose screens
were smashed and whose insides had been
ripped out.

Had he got the value of TVs all wrong? While he was turning this puzzle over in his mind, he found that he had become part of the red team – even though his T-shirt was so old it didn't really have a colour any more – who had formed a chain and were passing the boxes of food from the back of the truck all the way to the hut.

As Chipo took and passed on box after box, he introduced himself to the children next to him in the chain. "Hi," he said cheerily to the boy to his right. "I'm Chipo."

The boy scowled and shoved another box into Chipo's hands.

"Don't talk so loud!" the girl next to him scolded. She pointed at the boy. "He's called Sule, but he doesn't talk much."

Chipo handed her the next box.

"Only been here six months, but he's been

unlucky," she said quietly as he leaned close.

Chipo wondered what she meant. Sule did look a bit unlucky, with his scaly skin and bald head, and his blue, milky eyes that didn't seem to see very much.

"Shut up about unlucky, Ada," Sule said in a growling whisper. "Nothing unlucky about me. My last boss beat me and locked me in a box when I wasn't working. I'm lucky since I came here. Nobody beats me and I get fed."

Chipo took another box from him and passed it to Ada.

"I'm sorry," Ada said to Sule. "I just meant your skin, you know, and your eyes. Doesn't usually happen for a year or more. I mean, my lumps didn't start till the last rains, and I'd been here for two years by then."

Chipo felt a chill go through his body: Ada's skin was covered in knobbles and bumps, so big that it was hard to see where her nose and mouth were hidden in the landscape of her face. But she had not been born like this; it had happened to her after she came to Tortu's camp! Chipo passed several more boxes along in silence while his brain soaked up the information. At last, as calmly as he could, he asked, "Ada, what gives you the milky eyes and the lumps?"

"See what your chat has started, Ada?" hissed Sule. "You'd better shut up. If Tortu hears you there'll be trouble."

Ada bit her lumpy lip, and as Chipo leaned towards her to pass on the next box she whispered, "We think it's the water, and the stuff in the TVs. Poison."

Tortu's voice boomed across from the TV hills: "Work, don't talk, red team!"

After that, neither Sule nor Ada would say another word.

When it got really hot, the children were given a break. Everyone went inside the hut, where there was food and clean water to drink, all laid out on the long table. In all his life Chipo had never eaten three meals in one day; he had always gone hungry, sometimes very, very hungry, every day. Yet the sight of the food and water on the table just made him think of Ada's face and Sule's sightless eyes. He took just a few sips of water and went to Gentle's bunk.

She was *still* asleep, although Mouse opened one eye to look at Chipo, then closed it again. He sat on the side of the bunk looking at her, worrying. If what Ada said was right, then Tortu and his gang had been normal when they first arrived, and living in this camp somehow poisoned them and made them into . . . well, Chipo didn't want to say the word to himself, but he knew he was thinking *monsters*. And what else did living here do? He remembered Eric's words: *Could be that dying quick-quick is better than slow-slow, the way all of us is dying*. Were the children dying? Was that why there was no one here older than twelve or thirteen, except for Tortu himself? Chipo shuddered.

One by one, the children finished their meal, and went to their bunks to sleep away the heat. Soon there was no sound but the droning of the flies, and the children's coughs and snuffles.

But Chipo lay awake, watching: Tortu lying like a guard dog at the door of the hut, with his eyes darting about; poor Eric, wheezing in his bunk, unconscious, too sick to speak ever again. He watched and watched, and questions raced around his head without answers.

Chapter 13

Chipo was given a bright new T-shirt to wear and sent out with the yellow team. He was made to spend his days on the TV mound, smashing open TVs and pulling out their insides. It was horrible: tiny flecks of glass and plastic worked their way into his skin and made his hands and arms itch and blister, and the smashed TVs gave off a horrible bitter smell that made him cough. In the sun, the swamp seemed to breathe out too, sometimes sending a pinkish smog to wrap around the children as they laboured on the TV mountains. All the time Chipo thought about poison going into his body.

The other children didn't speak to him at all. He wondered if Tortu had told them not to, or if they just wanted to keep away from him. They certainly watched him, as if they were waiting for something. Chipo guessed what it was: they were waiting for the first sign that he was changing, turning into one of them. It filled him with a mixture of horror for himself and pity for them.

Every night he checked his skin anxiously, and looked at Gentle for any sign of lumps or scales. If any of the children smiled at him he couldn't help flinching, fearing that they had spotted some tiny sign or skin blemish that meant he was doomed like them.

Tortu watched him too, just as he watched

all the children, as if they were scorpions that might at any moment need to be squished. It gave Chipo goose bumps.

In fact he was so thoroughly unhappy that the food and the comfortable bunk began to mean nothing to him. All he could think about was how to get away. The moment Gentle was well enough, escape was the only option.

But Gentle was taking a long time to get better. It was a week before she managed to walk as far as the table with his help; another two days before she ate anything – although that *was* a whole packet of sweet biscuits.

"I like it here," she told Chipo sleepily. "No one minds my split face and there's lots to eat."

Chipo didn't say anything. There was no reason to worry her before he had a proper plan, but he made sure she drank only tinned fruit juice, not the water from the tap in the hut.

Mouse didn't like it there
either. In spite of being patted
and fussed and fed by the
monster children, she spent
as little time outside as
possible, and whined
when Chipo got ready
to go out each morning.
Chipo wondered if her
sensitive doggy nose

had told her all the secrets of Tortu's horrible
kingdom. She guarded Gentle constantly and
was incredibly pleased when Chipo returned to
the hut at the end of each day.

Out on the TV mound, with no one to talk
to or keep him company, Chipo had a lot of
time to watch and to think. He noticed that,
once children began to cough, they didn't get
better; he noticed that the scales and lumps

117

and milky eyes got worse, and as they got worse, some children were given a new colour T-shirt. Sule's coughing had been very bad one day, and the next morning Tortu stopped him at the door of the hut and gave him a white T-shirt. In spite of the fact that this meant easier work – cleaning the hut and preparing food – Sule looked very upset.

The truth was horrible to see – Tortu's kingdom changed the children into monsters, and then it made them very sick or even killed them. And even if it didn't kill them – Tortu himself seemed well enough and was clearly much older than anyone else – once they had begun to be monsters they were trapped. Having seen the way Gentle and her split face had been treated out in the world, Chipo knew that the only safe place for these lizard-like children was here. It wasn't only the electric fence and the poisoned swamp that kept them in.

He and Gentle and Mouse must leave – and soon, before the poison in the air and water did its deadly work. But he couldn't work out how – until the night when poor Eric died.

Chipo had been lying awake, trying to think quick about escaping. Amid the wheezes and coughs of the other children, he heard a long, low sigh from Eric's bunk. He had never heard anyone leave life before, but all the same he was certain that this was what had happened.

Tortu had heard it too. Chipo saw his dark shape uncurl and scuttle silently across the room and up to Eric's bunk. With a shudder, Chipo realized that Tortu must have had plenty of practice at carrying bodies, because he got Eric's out of his bunk in seconds. This, of course, was the next team that children joined after the white T-shirts. But what would

Tortu do with the body? Perhaps an escape for a corpse could be an escape for Chipo, Gentle and Mouse too.

Tortu was carrying Eric on his back. The boy's legs dangled and dragged on the floor for a moment, and Chipo was sure that some of the other children could hear what was going on. But perhaps they didn't want to listen. They must have seen other children die many times before. Or maybe Tortu punished children who were too curious. Chipo didn't really care. He waited until Tortu was at the door of the hut, struggling with his burden, then he slipped out of his bunk like a shadow. Keeping out of Owiti's way had made Chipo very good at moving without a sound.

Outside, a low half-moon lit up the surface of the swamp. Tortu was already out on the water: there was the silhouette of a little boat –

a dugout canoe, Chipo thought – with Tortu's hump in the middle of it, and another shape that must be Eric. As he watched, Tortu slid Eric's body into the water with a splash; there was a second splash, which Chipo guessed must be a weight to take Eric to the bottom. A moment later the boat was moving back towards the shore, with Tortu's hump dipping first one way and then the other as he paddled. Chipo watched as Tortu slid the narrow little craft into a hole in the bank, covering the opening with a piece of old tin.

Chipo hurried back to his bunk and lay quite still, listening as Tortu curled up in the doorway once more. He'd found their escape route, but there was one more problem: Gentle couldn't walk more than a few metres. How would he get her out of her bunk and into that dugout without another pair of hands?

Chapter 14

The next morning Chipo woke late. Everyone else was already up, and Tortu was calling: "Trucks, trucks. Everyone outside!"

Chipo scrambled down from his bunk and was swept out of the hut with the rest of the yellow team before he could even check on Gentle and Mouse. No one was taking any notice of Eric's empty bunk.

There were more boxes to load than to unload, so Tortu told Chipo to get into the back of the truck while the other yellows got the crates of TV innards ready for loading. There was a particularly horrible smog coming from the swamp, so Chipo was glad to jump up onto the truck, where the air was a bit cleaner, and move crates about.

As he dragged and carried, he wondered: Would it be better to try to escape in the middle of the night or the middle of the midday sleep? Where would they go in the canoe? Did the waters of the swamp lead anywhere else apart from back to the rubbish-burning electricity station? In fact, Chipo was so busy planning and thinking that he didn't notice that one of the boxes behind him had grown a pair of small feet and was moving towards him. So when the walking box bumped into him, he fell over in pure surprise. The top of the box opened, and a familiar head with a very familiar smile poked out of it.

"Dede!"

"Chipo!"

Dede was tangled up in the cardboard so
Chipo helped him to get free, then asked,
"How did you get here?"

"I was hungry," Dede said, "so I looked for
food in the empty boxes at the back of the
shop in Rubbish Town . . . and I fell asleep."
He shrugged and smiled, as if falling asleep
in a box and being scooped up by mistake
and landing who knows where was the most
natural thing in the world. Chipo felt like
laughing for the first time in days.

124

"Where is this?" asked Dede, looking around. "Are we in the city?"

Chipo didn't know what to say. The truth was, he wasn't sure *where* they were apart from in Tortu's kingdom. "It's another dump," he answered, "only specially for TVs."

Dede grinned. "A good place for you then, Chipo. I heard from Owiti that you like TVs!"

Chipo looked at his feet. "I'm not sure I like TVs so much now," he said, but there was no time to explain any more – the rest of the yellow team had arrived with their crates, ready to load up.

Tortu accepted Dede's arrival without question. Chipo guessed that children must regularly arrive like that – in the back of trucks, by mistake, or picked up from roadsides; maybe even sold by their families when times were rough. Children turned up on Fudu's work teams that way, so it was probably the same here.

Tortu's children stared at Dede as they had stared at Chipo and Gentle, but Dede seemed completely unconcerned by their strange appearance. Perhaps he was just too hungry to even notice, Chipo thought. At midday break, while Dede ate, within earshot of the others Chipo chatted to him about what a good place this was, with easy work and lots of food. Dede didn't say a word, but when he had finished eating, he played a tune on his whistle, and even Tortu went to his rest smiling; Dede had put everyone a little more at ease and seemed so relaxed himself that Chipo wondered how to explain that Tortu's dump was really a nightmare that they must escape from as soon as possible.

Chipo introduced Dede to Gentle, who

was asleep, and to Mouse, who wasn't. Mouse licked Dede's hand and made him giggle, and Chipo felt sure that when Gentle was awake she would like Dede as much as Mouse did.

They climbed into Chipo's bunk together and lay down, at opposite ends, to rest. Chipo waited until he was sure the other children and Tortu were asleep, and then wriggled his way to Dede's end of the bunk. Halfway there he found Dede was doing the same thing!

"Chipo," Dede breathed in the world's smallest whisper, "what's wrong with those kids? There's something funny about this place, isn't there?"

Clapping Dede on the back would have made way too much noise, but that's what Chipo wanted to do. "Dede, you are a lot cleverer than you look," he whispered. "You're right. And that's why we're getting out of here!"

Chapter 15

With the noise of smashing TVs to cover up their voices, Chipo had told Dede all about Tortu and Eric, about the children, the boat and his escape plan. Chipo knew it wasn't a great plan, but Dede had said, "We can't stay here, Chipo – every day we stay we might start changing."

Chipo knew he was right. All the same, setting off in a boat without having the first idea where you were going was as mad as Gentle's Happy Split-face Land. And Chipo worried about the children they were leaving behind. He knew they could all end up like Eric but he couldn't think of a way to take them too. And even if he could, Chipo wasn't sure they would come. Dede was right: there was no point waiting any longer, now that he was here to help with the escape plan.

So a few hours later, the friends crept past the snoring Tortu and hurried along the shore of the swamp in the darkness. Gentle was better at walking than Chipo had expected and just needed a little support from Dede on one side and Chipo on the other. She and Dede had taken to each other instantly.

"You know," Gentle told Dede, "I'm so glad we're leaving. The food was nice but I never liked it here. Mouse never liked it."

Mouse, padding along behind, trying to be quiet like her mistress and masters, gave a low

"Uff!" in agreement.

Keeping low and dodging behind TVs dumped in the mud, Chipo, Dede, Gentle and Mouse moved along the shore to where the canoe was hidden. They crouched behind a little drift of TVs and watched to make sure that no one had followed them, but the faint moonlight showed that they were alone.

The canoe was a bit bigger than it had looked from a distance, a solid dugout big enough for all four of them. Chipo was relieved; he'd been worried that it wouldn't take all of them and the packets of biscuits and tins of juice they'd smuggled along too. Chipo knew they'd have to eat and drink something on their journey but it wouldn't be tap water from Tortu's hut.

He and Dede pulled the boat out of its muddy hole and got it floating. None of the children had any experience of boats, and only Mouse seemed at home when the craft wobbled uncontrollably and threatened to tip them all out into the deadly poison of the swamp. But at last, with Mouse in the stern, Gentle in the prow, and Chipo and Dede in the middle holding a paddle each, the little craft settled down.

The boys pushed the canoe out onto the water, but they were still within arm's reach of the sticky shore when Gentle cried out, "Look! Tortu!"

She was right. A fast-moving hump was tracking their progress along the line of mud and stranded TVs. Tortu was running ahead of them on three of his four limbs, carrying something long and thin in one hand. He climbed up onto a little raised hummock, his strange shape clear in the moonlight, and called out to them.

"Don't think you can get away!" he rumbled, lifting up what he had been carrying: it was a long pole with a very nasty-looking hook on the end. Dede and Chipo were not yet good at steering, and their little boat was heading straight for where Tortu's pole poked out over the water. They couldn't avoid it, so the only thing to do was grab it and pull. Tortu wouldn't want to fall in, and they might be able to make him let go.

"Dede," said Chipo, "as soon as the pole touches us, we have to get hold of it."

Closer and closer they edged, the canoe moving sluggishly with its heavy load, so that the whole scene happened in a kind of slow motion.

At last they were level with Tortu's pole, and he gave a sudden jab that would have holed the canoe if Dede hadn't wrapped himself around

the hook and held on. The canoe tipped wildly.
Gentle screamed, Mouse yelped, and for a
moment it looked like they were all going to
be tipped into the swamp.

Chipo put down his paddle and began to
pull on the pole with Dede, but Tortu was
only drawing them closer to the bank, where
he could grab the canoe. He was holding on
with both arms now, and Chipo noticed that
standing on just his legs, he was a little wobbly.
Chipo had an idea. He whispered to Dede,
"When I say *Now*, push hard, then let go."

For another few seconds Chipo let Tortu

think he had won, then he hissed to Dede, "Now!"

The boys shoved the pole as hard as they could and immediately let go. Tortu overbalanced and fell backwards, and the canoe moved in the opposite direction. In a moment they were out of reach of the pole.

"Wow!" said Gentle. "Quick-thinking, fast-moving Chipo."

Chipo and Dede took up their paddles again, and the canoe began to speed up and pull away from the shore.

Tortu didn't yell in anger, or throw stones or bits of TV at them. Instead he ran along the shoreline, calling out to them, "Where are you going?" He sounded sad and worried rather than angry.

"Away from here!" Dede called back defiantly.

"But it's dangerous – the boat may sink; you don't know where you'll end up. You're only kids! Here it's safe."

"I'd rather face danger than die here," Chipo said proudly (a line he had to admit he'd stolen from Powerbolt – at least in part).

"Yes," shouted Dede. "I don't want to end up like that Eric!"

"But *I* didn't die," Tortu cried. "I've been here for years."

He suddenly sounded so lost, so forlorn, that Chipo's heart went out to him, and he shouted out, "Then come with us! Bring all the children."

"It's too late – too late . . ." Tortu's voice faded into the breeze that had begun to blow more strongly, carrying them away, so that he was soon just a part of the dark shoreline.

Chapter 16

The wind pushed them like a friendly hand, away from the TV mountain, and then beyond the warehouse and its sparking web of wires. They were no longer on a swamp, but floating faster and faster down a river that carried them along so swiftly, paddling was soon irrelevant. Chipo told Dede to rest, and used the paddle simply to steer, watching out for obstacles in the water and avoiding collisions. There was time for talking. Chipo told Gentle all he knew about Tortu and the children; how the swamp and the poisons from the TVs changed them; how Eric had died, probably the way many other children before him had died. They too would surely have ended up in the swamp if they'd stayed.

Gentle's brow furrowed. "What I don't understand is, why don't the children escape as soon as they know what might happen to them?"

Chipo shook his head. "I think they come from places where they've been starved, or beaten like Sule, so all they want is to be fed and safe. Then they start to change, and then they're stuck, 'cos they're almost blind like Sule, or they look like lizards and they'd be chased away from anywhere else, even Rubbish Town. And anyway," he added, "you should have seen the electric fence around that place. Anyone trying to get out would be fried."

"Do you think we'll go scaly, Chipo?" Gentle asked.

He answered as quickly as he could so he'd sound convincing. "No, course not. You'd have to be there for years to get enough poison for that."

Gentle didn't need to know about Sule losing his sight in just six months, or how the clouds of pink fog had wrapped around Chipo for days on end on the TV mounds.

"We were lucky to get away," she said.

"Nothing to do with luck, little sister." Chipo grinned. "All the doing of your superhero brother."

Gentle laughed and rolled her eyes, and for a while they fell silent. Dede played his whistle, and the sweet sad sound threaded its way over the water, along with Chipo's thoughts about the monster children and Tortu.

138

At last Dede fell asleep and Gentle curled up in the prow. Chipo was alone on the river.

"I wish," he said quietly to himself, "I *wish* that I could have helped all those children we've left behind."

To his surprise, Gentle stirred. "You will, Chipo," she said softly. "You will. I know it."

In the dark she sounded so grown up. Chipo found he had a lump in his throat that stopped him from saying anything at all for quite a while.

The river carried them on but Chipo couldn't sleep. He stopped thinking about what they had left behind, and began to think about what was in front of them. He looked at the lines of wires and pylons beside the river, carrying all that important electricity. It was clear that both river and electricity were going to the same place, and in such a place there would be great opportunities for a quick-thinking, fast-moving person. Chipo felt as if they were being carried exactly where he wanted them to go, as if a great future was opening out in front of them.

Eventually, even his great plans couldn't keep him awake, and he drooped over his paddle and slept.

He woke in bright sunshine to the noise of a very cross-sounding siren and a loud voice saying, "No pleasure craft are allowed in the dam zone. No pleasure craft are allowed in the dam zone."

They were in the middle of a wide, very calm stretch of river. Buildings, warehouses, cranes, and all the equipment of a big river port stood on both banks, with taller buildings forming the skyline beyond. They had reached the important place, Chipo guessed, where all that electricity was going – the city!

A motorboat with all sorts of flags and shiny bits of metal on it was coming towards them. Before they'd had time to wake up properly they found themselves being dragged from the canoe, pulled onto the deck of the motorboat, and made to stand in front of a hugely fat man in a uniform with a lot of gold buttons.

"I am Captain Odwalay," he said, as if he was announcing that he was King of the Universe. Then he asked, "Who are you?" Chipo thought he might have spoken to cockroaches in a nicer way.

"I am Chipo," he said, being as charming as possible just to set Captain Odwalay a good example of how superheroes speak to strangers. "And this is my sister, Gentle, my friend, Dede, and our dog and family member, Mouse."

In spite of Chipo having made an effort to

be as polite as possible, Captain Odwalay still looked very cross.

"I mean," he said, even more loudly, "who *are* you? What is your position? Are you a fisherman? Are you a ferryman? Or is this canoe of yours a purely recreational craft?"

Chipo made himself wake up a bit more. This was obviously not going to be easy. He looked at Gentle, who had hurriedly wrapped her bandage round her face again, but she shrugged. He looked at Dede, who smiled his most charming smile and said nothing. He looked at Mouse, who uffed at him in mystification.

"Well," Chipo began slowly, "I'm not a fisherman, and I'm not a ferryman, but I don't think I'm that other thing you said either. We were escaping."

"Escaping?" said the man, raising his

eyebrows so high they disappeared under his peaked cap.

"Yes," Chipo repeated. "Escaping."

"Oh!" The captain looked much less cross, but even more as though he had a nasty smell under his nose. "Refugees! I see."

Refugees, Chipo guessed, were a bit worse than cockroaches as far as men with gold buttons were concerned.

The captain brought a huge rubber stamp down on the paper in front of him with such a bang that all three of them jumped. He handed the paper to Chipo, told a man with rather fewer gold buttons, "Get them off my ship!" and walked off.

"Can we have our canoe back?" Chipo called after him. A canoe, after all, might be useful even in a big city.

Captain Odwalay didn't even bother to turn

round. "Your 'canoe'," he said, "has been sunk. It was a health hazard."

Half an hour later, Chipo, Gentle, Dede and Mouse were standing on a wharf. On one side of them were ships bigger than all of Rubbish Town put together, tied up with giant ropes to enormous metal rings and bollards. And on the

other, skyscrapers, warehouses, shops, shacks,
kiosks, roads, traffic lights, cars, people, bustle
and chaos stretched out for what looked
like infinity. They had arrived! This was the
place where all that electricity was leading; the
place where all the trash of Rubbish Town and
the TVs of Tortu's little kingdom came from.
The very first city any of them had ever seen.

It was terrifying!

Chipo's mouth dropped open. He suddenly felt very small indeed; all his great plans and his quick-thinking-fast-moving-ness seemed to trickle out of the soles of his feet onto the concrete. Dede's smile faded like a wilted flower, and Gentle needed to lean against Chipo so as not to fall down. There were so many new sights and sounds – and, for Mouse, new smells – that it was impossible to make sense of what lay before them. The four companions stood huddled together like mice before a convention of cats, not knowing where to go or what to do.

But big and dangerous cities, as this one was, have a way of herding little people like Chipo, Dede and Gentle, because the people who *do* know where to go and what to do are always telling the ones who *don't* to get out of the way. This began to happen almost at once: dockers loading cargo onto the big ships pushed and bullied them away from the wharf; cars zooming down the roads made them jump for safety; busy workers rushing along the pavements sent them in search of quieter streets; beggars and dealers harried and frightened them into alleys and doorways.

Chipo held Dede's hand in his left hand and Gentle's in his right, and tried to be as brave as possible, but Mouse was really their protector, growling and snarling at any sign of threat, so they never came to any harm. They moved on through the city, like flour being sifted through different grades of sieve, until they came to some shanties and shacks, built among the bombed-out ruins of grand old houses, where other people like them had ended up; people whom the city had sifted slowly and surely down to the very bottom.

At the end of the day, dazed and exhausted, hungry and discouraged, they fled the noise and bustle, and found themselves in an overgrown courtyard surrounded by ruined houses, whose big doorways were still intact. One of these looked like a safe place to spend a night. Chipo was just getting Gentle and Dede settled, and wondering if it was better to go hungry or eat the food they'd brought from Tortu's dump, when a pair of dusty pink sandals, with a pair of wide feet inside, stamped the ground in front of him. Chipo looked up to see a large lady in a robe and headdress that matched her sandals. She had several huge bundles strapped to her back, and she didn't look pleased.

"What do you think you are doin' in *my* doorway?" she demanded.

"I'm sorry," Chipo said. "I didn't know

it was yours." He got up wearily and began gathering their small store together.

"Yes," added Dede, his sunflower smile reviving a little. "Yes, we're really sorry."

"Sorry," Gentle added in her funny little voice from behind her bandage. Mouse wagged her tail weakly.

The woman's face lost its scowl. She smiled. "Well," she said. "Good manners! There's something I haven't met for quite a while. I am Miss Pink, and I'm pleased to meet you. This is my doorway, and that one over there is used by Mr Calabash." She pointed to where a tall skinny man was unloading his load of calabashes – pots and bowls of all shapes and sizes made from dried gourds. He raised a hand in greeting at them.

"He has his faults," whispered Miss Pink behind her hand, "but he is a respectable person.

The door next to that," she went on in a normal voice, "should suit you just fine. I'll be brewing a little tea shortly – I'll bring you some!"

The children moved round to the doorway Miss Pink had suggested, passing Mr Calabash on the way; he came out and shook their hands and Mouse's paw.

"Fortitude Calabash, that's me," he said. "Always pleased to meet young people." He dropped his voice and whispered behind his hand, just as Miss Pink had done, "I see you've met the lady over there. She has her faults, but she's a decent old bird really."

Chipo, Gentle and Dede nodded, and then remembered that it might be a good idea to close their mouths, even though they were so astonished. None of them had ever met grown-ups who were so warm and friendly, and so funny.

Their new doorway wasn't as big or as smooth as Miss Pink's, but it was better, Chipo thought, than the bottom of their crater back in Rubbish Town. They ate crackers and drank water, and Mouse went and sniffed around in the undergrowth covering the old courtyard and came back with a nice dead rat to chew on. In a little while Miss Pink came over with an enamel cup of hot tea for them to share, and Mr Calabash brought some fried yam – left over, he said, from his lunch. They sat together as it grew dark, and chatted.

"Calabash by name and by business," said Mr Calabash. "I make 'em and I sell 'em."

"I'm a fashion retailer myself," said Miss Pink, patting her headdress, "although both Mr Calabash and I are waiting for the car bombs to stop so the street market will open again."

"So . . ." Mr Calabash smiled. "How do you

youngsters plan on making a living in this city?"

Dede spoke up at once, looking more and more like his old self. "I'm going to be a musician!" He played a little phrase on his whistle to demonstrate. Miss Pink and Mr Calabash looked impressed and exchanged a knowing look.

"What about you?" Mr Calabash asked, turning his smile on Chipo.

After the day they'd had, Chipo really didn't have any plans left. Saving monster children? Trading in TV intestines? He ran a few replies through his head, but none seemed very good. He could see that Gentle was having similar thoughts about washing out dustbin bags; she would be a great witch impersonator, but only for emergencies, as people were very, very scared of witches. It was a shame Mouse couldn't talk because dead rat disposal was always a useful profession no matter where you went. Mouse noticed Chipo looking at her and wagged her tail, and at that moment a thought suddenly popped into his head, and he couldn't imagine why he hadn't thought of it before.

"Our dog," he said, "is very special. I'm going to train her to do tricks and she will earn us lots of money."

Dede clapped his hands and beamed. "That's a great idea, Chipo!" he said.

But Gentle was not so impressed; luckily, where Miss Pink and Mr Calabash were sitting they couldn't see just how much she was rolling her eyes.

Chapter 17

Over the next few days Chipo came to understand that there were many, many kinds of bad luck to be had in the city. There were thieves and muggers, knife gangs and cruel police officers; there were trucks that didn't care who they hit, and even car bombs and gunfire, as the war that had killed Chipo's parents had never quite died away here. But amid so much that could go wrong, finding this courtyard, Miss Pink and Mr Calabash was the most amazing piece of the very best kind of good luck.

Miss Pink and Mr Calabash spent at least the start and end of every day, and every night, in their doorways, and they were very pleased to have such polite and charming new neighbours as Chipo and his family. They were so pleased, in fact, that they looked out for them in all sorts of ways – from bringing them a mug of tea or a bit of fried yam, to giving them information: which streets were safe and which were not; where to get clean water from a tap; where there was a bath house to shower and wash your clothes; which street food sellers were the best and cheapest; and where poor people could get free food.

It was clear too that Dede had adopted Chipo, Gentle and Mouse as his own family. Of the three children he was the one who settled most quickly into city life.

"I'm like a fish who has reached the sea," he

told them, his eyes shining. "Now I must swim and grow strong!"

Mr Calabash showed Dede the best street corners for budding musicians, so his playing was already earning a little money, which he was eager to share with Chipo and Gentle. When Chipo tried to thank him, he said, "Remember the coil of wire, Chipo? Fudu would have pushed me out like a cockroach if it wasn't for you. *You* never need to thank *me*."

Gentle too found her place in their new life. Miss Pink needed help with her business – washing and mending clothes.

"It's just like washing bin bags!" Gentle said happily. "Miss Pink says when the street markets start up again, when the car bombs stop, she'll pay me!"

But Chipo took longer to get used to the city. The sounds of sirens, screams, explosions and guns in the night kept him awake, and he felt bad that he didn't seem to have a way of making a living as Dede and Gentle had. He was supposed to be the big brother: where were all his plans and schemes?

One problem was that turning Mouse into a performing dog did not go well. As soon as Chipo started trying to get her attention, ready to begin training, she would simply lie down with a huge sigh and go to sleep.

Gentle thought this was very funny. "You're just not interesting enough, Chipo," she teased.

Dede was, as always, encouraging. "Keep trying, Chipo. I know you'll get her to learn tricks."

"Maybe not, Dede," said Miss Pink. "Maybe that dog is just too stupid to learn!"

"Maybe you need to beat her to make her

learn," Mr Calabash joked, and Gentle put her arms round Mouse's neck and pretended to glare at him.

Of course, Chipo had no plans to beat Mouse. Mouse was their protection against many kinds of the city's bad luck; no thief, mugger or gang would take on Mouse when she began to snarl. Chipo hoped she'd learn tricks in time; right now, she was an essential part of their family. Gentle had recovered from the poison of the swamp but now had an infection in her ears and a fever. Chipo had to leave her behind when he went to fetch water or food or look for a job. Dede, Miss Pink and Mr Calabash were often out on the streets trying to earn some money, so Gentle was all alone, and Mouse seemed to understand that it was her duty to take care of her while Chipo went searching for opportunity.

Opportunity was hard to find, especially standing in long queues, waiting to fill their water bottle from a tap, or to get a handout of free food. Chipo didn't find much of it when he knocked on the doors of shops and houses asking for work, either. The car bombs and gunfire had made people nervous, so many didn't come to their doors, and every time there was any kind of bang, people screamed and dived for cover. Several times Chipo lost his place in a queue when he was almost at the front, because a car door had slammed and everyone had panicked and run off. For days, all he had to bring back to Gentle and Mouse was water and a bit of cooked rice, wrapped in a leaf. If it hadn't been for Dede's money and the food that Miss Pink and Mr Calabash shared with them, Chipo's family would have been very hungry indeed.

And then, just when Chipo was least expecting it, he bumped right into opportunity. He'd been walking all morning and he was feeling a bit wobbly, so he stepped out of the hot sun into the shade of the side street. But his eyes did not adjust quickly enough to the change from bright light to deep shade and he blundered into something that clattered to the ground with a sound like the end of the universe. For a moment Chipo was sure he had been blown up and was dead. When he found that he wasn't in bits and his eyes got accustomed to the gloom, he saw that he hadn't been caught in an explosion but had knocked over a huge pile of baking tins. If he hadn't been so tired he might have just run away, but instead he began to pick them up.

"What you do with my bake tins?" an angry voice demanded.

Chipo looked up to see a small man in a big white apron standing in a doorway. "I walked into them," he said. "I'm sorry, I'll pile them up again."

"Hmm," said the man with his hands on his hips. He stood watching while Chipo carefully picked up the tins and made them into a neat stack. "Those tins are my big problem," the man sighed. "Always need cleaning, but I don't have time."

Chipo froze in the middle of his stacking and looked at the man, and the man looked back. Then they both smiled, recognizing in each other a solution to both their problems.

"I'll clean them for you!" said Chipo.

"Yes!" The man beamed. "Yes, you will!"

So that was how Chipo got a job at Mr Atee's bake shop on Astove Street. The next morning, before it was light, he set off across town feeling like a different boy. He was the head of his family once again, no longer dependent on the charity of friends. The streets were already quite busy with other workers, walking determinedly to early jobs. It made Chipo feel very grown up to be part of this special group of people who would be earning their pay while most of the city – including Dede, Gentle, Miss Pink and Mr Calabash – was still just dreaming.

He arrived at the back door of the bakery just as Mr Atee was turning the loaves out of their metal tins, and then for two hours Chipo scrubbed and scrubbed those tins until they shone.

"So clean, Chipo," Mr Atee exclaimed, delighted. "So bright they reflect the sun!"

Chipo ran almost all the way home with his pay, bought roasted plantain and fried yams for everyone's breakfast, and proudly distributed them to the sleepy courtyard residents on his return.

With Mr Atee's money to buy better food, Gentle's health improved; her ears stopped hurting, although Chipo noticed she didn't hear as well as before. But of course when he had to repeat something that her ears had missed, it was always *his* fault.

"You've stopped talking properly since we

came to the city," she'd say. "You mumble like an old man, Chipo!"

Chipo didn't mind; he was just glad she was better. So he'd wink at Dede when she scolded, and Dede would wink back.

Gentle did more and more for Miss Pink. Miss Pink showed her how to do embroidery. At first she just filled in her bandage map drawings with stitching, but then she moved on to embroider her own designs onto little cloths that Miss Pink was going to sell for her. Chipo was delighted. At last Gentle would stop thinking about Happy Split-face Land and school, and get some more practical dreams – like his own newest ambition:

"I'm going to have a bakery," he said to himself, "just like Mr Atee's!"

Chapter 18

Chipo's job at Mr Atee's made him feel that everything was going to go well from now on. The city itself seemed to be getting better. He was sure there were fewer explosions and bursts of gunfire in the night. Mr Calabash thought so too.

"All getting back to normal!" he said. "You'll see!"

The one thing that wasn't going better was Mouse's training. Every morning when he got back from Mr Atee's, Chipo gave Mouse a "lesson". But no matter what he did, she didn't seem able to concentrate for more than a few seconds before she was nipping fleas on her bottom, or chasing a fly. She wouldn't "sit" or "stay", or even listen to a single thing Chipo said to her. He was ready to give up.

Then, one morning, he came home with a little bag of pastry bits that he had scraped off the tins, tucked into his back pocket. The moment Mouse smelled them, it was as if her nose was glued to his shorts, and she began to make a sort of high wailing sound!

"What's in your pocket?" asked Gentle.

"Burned pastry!" Chipo laughed. He pulled the bag out of his pocket, and Mouse followed the move as if the bag and her nose were joined by a string, her voice going round with her nose like a little police siren. It was so funny!

"Wave it around a bit." Dede giggled. "See

what she'll do!"

Chipo held the bag high above his head, then
swung it down to the ground, around and up
again. Mouse was hypnotized. Chipo broke off
a tiny piece of pastry and held it in front of her.

"Sit!" he said. Mouse sat, still whining a
little. Chipo rewarded her with the titbit, and
her expression made him, Dede and Gentle
laugh out loud. Never, said Mouse's quivering
nose and half-closed eyes, never in all her life
of chewing rat bones and licking out empty
tins at the Old Dump had she ever even
dreamed of anything so delicious.

From that moment Mouse's training went
very well indeed. Every day Mr Atee gave
Chipo a few pastry scraps, and every day, when
he got home from the bakery, Chipo would
spend hours working with Mouse. By the end
of the first week she could sit, lie down and

roll over. By the end of two weeks' training she could walk on her hind legs, jump over a stick that Chipo held out, and lift one paw to shake hands.

It was Dẹde's idea to teach Mouse to dance. "If she can stand on her hind legs and you can get her to sort of twirl," he said, "I can play so it sounds like she's doing it to the music."

At first it didn't go well. Mouse kept getting giddy and falling over after just a couple of turns. And then, when Chipo worked out that it was best to teach her to turn one way then the other to prevent this, it looked so funny that all three children would fall about laughing; then Mouse would think it was a game and the lesson would end in a pile of giggling children and wagging tail. But at last they had worked out a routine, and Dede had a jolly little tune that could be played fast or slow depending on how Mouse did her turns and jumps.

"It's really good!" Gentle said the first time they managed it all the way through without a mistake. "But why does she still make that awful noise when she smells the pastry?"

"I don't know," said Chipo, "but it'll just have to be part of the act."

"I'll think of something to play over the top," Dede suggested. However, this never quite worked out as he found Mouse's wailing so funny he was always laughing too much to play his whistle.

When Chipo told Mr Atee about the magical effect of his pastry scraps, he laughed so much that tears rolled down his cheeks, and he made his wife and daughter come and stand outside and hear the story again. When Chipo left, Mrs Atee gave him a whole pastry to take home.

"For you," she said, smiling shyly, "not the dog!"

Miss Pink and Mr Calabash both brought friends to see how well Mouse was doing.

"That dog may be smarter than we

thought," said Mr Calabash to his buddy, a little old man as wrinkly and silent as a walnut, "but she's still ugly!"

"You should take a look in the mirror before you call other persons ugly," Miss Pink called out to him, and her friend – who was neither wrinkly nor silent – cackled with laughter and shook her dangly earrings.

"No shame in being ugly," said Mr Calabash apologetically. "Take you, for instance, Mamma, you aren't 'shamed of being the ugliest lady on the streets!"

For some reason both Miss Pink and her friend and Mr Calabash and his friend seemed to find this very funny, and there was a full minute of laughter and no more speech. Dede, Gentle and Chipo looked at each other: grown-ups were just weird sometimes.

Miss Pink stopped laughing and said, "Time

that dog earned you some money, Chipo."

"And I'll play the music for her to dance to!" said Dede.

"Well," said Miss Pink. "Music and a dancing dog – could be good for us all, Mr Calabash. Get some extra customers, eh?"

Mr Calabash leaped up, snapping his fingers and pushing his hat forward at a jaunty angle. "Yes, yes!" he cried. "Liberty Street market is open again on Saturday – we'll all go down there together!"

"Now you're talking, old man!" said Miss Pink, clapping her hands and starting to dance in front of him.

"Who you callin' old?" Mr Calabash snapped back, and they both giggled again fit to burst.

Chapter 19

On Saturday morning, when Chipo got back from Astove Street, Gentle and Miss Pink were already up and fussing around Mouse.

"We're going to make her look pretty," Gentle said, her eyes smiling above the new flower-patterned veil that Miss Pink had made for her. She was wiping Mouse's grubby fur with a wet rag while Miss Pink tied a wide blue ribbon around the dog's neck.

"Blue," she said happily to Chipo. "Very good against her pale fur."

Chipo decided this was definitely women's stuff, so he went to look for Dede, who was often having a cup of tea in Mr Calabash's doorway at this time of the morning. But Dede wasn't there.

"Have you seen Dede this morning, Mr Calabash?" Chipo asked.

"Hmm . . . Dede," said Mr Calabash as if it was the first time he'd heard his name. "I'm not really certain. He'll probably join us later."

Chipo was mystified by this strange answer. He looked at Mr Calabash over his tea and wondered if he was quite well. Or perhaps Dede had found something better to do this morning than come and play for Mouse's dancing. Chipo drank his tea and tried not to feel hurt.

Over in the other doorway, Mouse was looking dejected,

with her tail between her legs and her one good ear droopy and sad-looking. She endured her beauty session until Miss Pink tried to put another blue ribbon on the end of her tail, and then she ran off to Mr Calabash. He scratched her head, then snatched the blue ribbon off her neck and waved it at Miss Pink, who rushed towards him, her hands on her hips.

"What are you doing?" she growled.

"Mamma," he said quietly, shaking his big lion head and taking off his hat to salute her, "you can't cure ugliness with clothes. This dog is like you: she will be a big success because of her brains, not her beauty." Very gently he touched Miss Pink's forehead with one long finger.

"Hmm!" said Miss Pink, pushing his finger to one side. "Get your wares together, old man. Let's go get these young people a good spot for their first performance."

Mr Calabash beamed. "Ready when you are, old woman."

In five minutes, the courtyard residents had packed away all their belongings and were walking down the alley in the slanting early sun towards Liberty Street.

Gentle was not quite well enough to manage the long walk, but as soon as she began to get tired, Mr Calabash put her in his barrow amongst the bowls and pots, so that her head stuck out above them like another kind of calabash.

As they walked, the streets around began to change, from dirt roads full of dust and potholes to smooth concrete highways, and wide, stone-flagged pavements that felt nice and soothing under Chipo's bare feet. The buildings changed too – from ruins patched up with bits of tin and plastic sheeting to shiny new skyscrapers. There were more bombed-out, blackened cars here – one on almost every street – and the brick and stone of the walls were spattered with bullet marks. But there were fewer and fewer rusty trucks and carts pulled by mules, and more and more swanky cars. There were still lots of people just like Chipo, dressed in clothes so old they'd lost all shape and colour and were more holes than material, but there were other sorts of people too: shiny, smart ones coming and going from the tall buildings and driving the swanky cars. Their clothes were so clean and bright they made Chipo's eyes hurt. He wondered if that was why so many of them were wearing sunglasses.

"Try not to stare, Chipo!" Miss Pink told him. "The rich people don't like it."

So Chipo stopped staring but decided he was going to have sunglasses too, so he could stare at whoever he wanted to without them knowing. He looked out for Dede at every corner, hoping that he would be waiting for them, but there was no sign of him.

Just as the sun was getting warm and the pavement was losing its early morning coolness, they arrived at a huge building, wider and taller than any Chipo had seen before. Growing along one long, long side of it was a row of bottle palms, casting round pools of shade almost as far as Chipo could see. And in every pool, someone seemed to be getting ready to sell something: fat mangoes piled in heaps, plates of little cakes, toy cars made from old drinks cans, chains for bicycles, tiny birds made from painted nut shells, strings of beads, clay pots big enough to hide in, rows of folded sarongs like chopped-up rainbows, plastic sandals, pineapples, wooden carvings. So many things, it made Chipo's head spin.

Mr Calabash cleared a path through the sellers and their goods with Gentle and the barrow. "Our spot is the tenth tree along, one of the biggest."

Chipo looked from Mr Calabash to Miss Pink, surprised that they shared anything considering how much they squabbled.

"We don't always share a spot," Miss Pink said quickly. "Just . . . sometimes."

"Just always," mumbled Mr Calabash.

They reached the tenth tree. Two lanky young men with very bright white trainers and mobile phones were hanging about in its shade, but Mouse snarled at them and they were gone in a moment.

"Huh!" said Mr Calabash. "I should bring this ugly dog every day. Would save me some time. Usually takes half an hour of talk-talk to get those boys to move."

Mr Calabash unloaded his calabashes, and Chipo helped him to arrange them in rows and little groups on coloured cloths. Miss Pink pulled a bundle of metal rods from a sack and fitted them together to make hanging rails. In minutes she had all her bundles of clothes hung up, like a real shop. She even had a folding chair and table so she could make a little counter. Between Mr Calabash's display and Miss Pink's clothes rails there was a nice shady space.

"This will be your stage!" said Miss Pink. "As soon as the street is busy, you can begin."

"I will be your announcer," said Mr Calabash, pointing importantly to his own chest. "I will call in people from all along Liberty Street."

"Quit your boasting, old man," said Miss Pink. "You have a customer!"

Chapter 20

It was a very busy morning. It had been a month since the last market, and people thronged the streets, catching up on lost shopping time. Once or twice a car backfired and a few people screamed – one or two even flattened themselves on the pavement – but when everyone realized it wasn't another bomb, or a gun going off, they just laughed.

"Look at that," said Mr Calabash as a lady got up from the ground and brushed off her dress. "She's smiling and laughing. Two weeks ago she'd have been running home and we would have lost a potential customer! Ah, we can put all that behind us now. The war is really over at last!"

All morning Chipo helped Mr Calabash with his customers. He showed them the different things that Mr Calabash had to sell, smiling his best smile and taking their money. Meanwhile Mr Calabash sat with his back against the tree, carving more gourds with patterns and making them into new bowls and pots. He grinned at Chipo. "We are a team, young man, a team!"

Although Gentle couldn't talk to customers or even hear much of what they said, Miss Pink let her stand on a chair and rearrange the clothes on the racks according to colour. Chipo could see that she was smiling behind her scarf, her earache all forgotten.

Mouse stretched out in the shade and slept. In fact everybody was enjoying themselves. Chipo tried to enjoy himself too, but he was sad and rather hurt that Dede wasn't going to be here to play for Mouse's debut, after all that practising.

At lunch time Liberty Street grew even busier. People filled the pavement and spilled over into the road, forcing the swanky cars to slow down.

"Now," declared Mr Calabash, "is your moment. Wake your dog. Get her treats ready and give this calabash to your sister so she can collect the money."

Mr Calabash threw a patched sheet over all his wares, to show that for the moment his stall was closed, and stood on top of his upturned barrow. "Friends and citizens," he bellowed, "sisters and brothers . . ."

His voice was very loud, but the crowd of people was noisier still and no one paid any attention to him. Rolling her eyes, Miss Pink stood up and gave the longest, loudest, highest ululation that Chipo had ever heard. It cut through the racket of people and cars like a knife. Gentle heard it and made a face as she stood on a chair to tidy up her brother's unruly hair.

"Are you going to put a blue ribbon round my neck?" Chipo asked her.

"Only if you want one." She grinned. "Good luck!"

Mr Calabash began again. "Friends, citizens, brothers and sisters, gather round for the first performance by Mouse the performing dog!"

Now people paid attention, so when Mr Calabash bowed low and stepped to one side to make a space for Chipo and Mouse, hundreds of eyes were looking at them. Chipo felt his mouth go dry and his head spin. He stood staring at the crowd with Mouse at his feet, scratching a flea behind her ear with a back leg. People laughed, and some began to move away looking very cross. Chipo felt he'd do better with a little musical introduction from his friend.

"Get on with it!" Mr Calabash hissed.

Music or no music, it was now or never. Chipo felt the little fragment of Mr Atee's pastry in his hand, and stood up as straight as he could. Mouse began her wailing in anticipation of the treat; the audience giggled nervously, not knowing what to expect from this funny-looking dog and her strange noises. Chipo realized he'd have to go straight for something spectacular to win them over.

"Mouse, jump high!" Chipo raised his arm

to show Mouse what he wanted her to do. They had been practising this trick a lot in the last few days and Mouse had got really good at jumping very high from a standing start. She leaped straight up into the air, so high that her back legs were higher than Chipo's head. It looked exactly as if someone had pushed her up from below. The fact that a moment before she had been lolling about like a sack of potatoes, with one leg behind her ear, made the transformation to canine rocket even more remarkable. The crowd loved it; they laughed out loud and cheered – and cheered even more when she did it a second time, and got even higher.

"Mouse, roll over!"

Mouse lay down with her head between her paws and rolled over and over like a rolled-up carpet.

"Mouse, leap!" Chipo commanded, and

crouched down to let Mouse jump backwards and forwards over him. She did it beautifully, and Chipo gave her an extra large chunk of pastry.

Now it was time for their most complicated trick – a series of moves where Mouse wove in and out of Chipo's legs as he walked forwards then backwards, and then stood on her back legs and twirled in time with Chipo like a dance partner. This was the part that Dede had offered to accompany. Chipo got up onto Mr Calabash's barrow and made a long announcement to give Mouse a rest and allow Dede a little more time to appear.

"Ladies and gentlemen, brothers and sisters," he said. "This dog is a very special dog, and to show you how special, I will now show you how she can dance!"

The crowed murmured in anticipation, but

from the very back came a loud child's voice.

"Stop!" it said. "Stop! Wait! You can't dance without music!"

The owner of the voice pushed through to the front, wiggling between the tightly packed people and then popping out between the forest of legs. It was Dede! And he was holding a beautiful new wooden flute, so big that it made him seem smaller than ever.

"Sorry I'm late. Had to pick up the flute!"

He grinned his wonderful opening-flower grin, and began to play.

The tune made some people start to clap along. Soon the whole crowd had joined in — men in suits and men in shorts and T-shirts, ladies in old cotton frocks and ladies with gold bangles and high headdresses — swaying to Dede's beat like a dancing rainbow. When Mouse finished twirling and hopping on her

hind legs, everyone cheered and clapped.
Chipo and Dede bowed low. Mouse ran up to
Gentle, her tail wagging in delight as if to say,
See how well I did!

And the coins fell into Gentle's calabash
like rain.

Chapter 21

Working together on Liberty Street, on
Mr Calabash's and Miss Pink's stalls, with
Mouse's tricks and Dede's playing, made a big
difference. It was as if Dede was the last piece
of a puzzle and now everyone fitted together.
Mr Calabash put it best:

"Before, we were just ingredients; now we
are a stew!"

Almost every day, Mouse performed at the
tenth tree on Liberty Street, with Mr Calabash
and Miss Pink as her announcers. Dede

accompanied the dancing part of Mouse's show on his whistle and then he played on his own. Dede admitted to Chipo that previously, when he played on his own, he had often had his earnings stolen because he was too little to stand up for himself. Now that never happened.

Gentle came too, riding in Mr Calabash's barrow, helping Miss Pink with the clothes and then collecting money for Chipo and Mouse and Dede. The coins filled her calabash, while Miss Pink and Mr Calabash sold more because of the crowds that came to see Mouse dance and hear Dede play.

In fact business was so good under the tenth tree that they managed to put their money together to rent a little tin house, round the corner from their old courtyard at the end of Palm Drive. Miss Pink took some persuading as she was not sure she wanted to live under the same roof as Mr Calabash, but when Chipo and Dede told her the house was on Rose Street and had three rooms, so she could have one all to herself, she agreed.

Their new home changed everything. Mr Calabash and Miss Pink no longer had to carry everything on their backs each time they went out; the tin house had a big fat padlock on the door, so it was safe to leave things there.

Mr Calabash mended the holes in the roof and made a little trench all around the outside of the house so that, now the rains had come, water couldn't get in, no matter how hard it tried. He put up a screen made of flattened cardboard boxes to make one room into two, and give their house three bedrooms, so that the middle room could be a place for everyone to share. They bought some chairs, and an old door for a table, and a fat round stove to cook on. It smoked so much they sometimes had to open the door, and Miss Pink complained that Mr Calabash hadn't put the chimney – made from old bean cans – in properly. But mostly it was just fine to have a stove to cook on and sit round on nights when the rains beat on the roof like somebody throwing handfuls of stones.

Living together in a house took a bit of getting used to. There were chores to be done, like remembering to buy millet for supper, or bring home charcoal to fuel the stove. At first they sometimes forgot, but Miss Pink made a rota of jobs, and soon the household was running smoothly. Gentle and Dede loved it. They never forgot their chores. But Chipo and Mr Calabash sometimes did. Chipo tried to make up for the fact that he didn't always fetch water when it was his turn by asking for some of his pay from Mr Atee in bread, so that everyone could start the day with some fresh bakes. Mr Calabash made up for the fact that he sometimes forgot to buy food on the way home by being the person who mended things when they were broken.

All in all, everyone got along fine – especially Mouse, who loved having a proper house to guard and would growl fiercely at the slightest sound outside. Inside their house they felt safe, even though the car bombs and shooting had started up again. Inside their house they were all calmer and there seemed to be more time for plans and dreams.

Miss Pink and Mr Calabash never seemed to fight any more. Miss Pink let Mr Calabash help carry her bundles of clothes, and Mr Calabash let Miss Pink mend his trousers. They took it in turns to cook dinner for everyone, so that every night the three children, the grown-ups and the dog gathered around the table. If business was good, it might be Mr Calabash's spicy chicken; if it was bad it might be Miss Pink's delicious fried plantains, or the groundnut stew they made together.

One night Miss Pink made groundnut stew *and* Mr Calabash made chicken yassa, and as everyone sat down at the table, Mr Calabash stood up and cleared his throat.

"I have something important to say." He glanced down at Miss Pink and she squeezed his hand. Dede and Chipo looked at each other and shrugged. What was going on? Gentle saw their bewildered faces and rolled her eyes.

"The important thing I have to say," Mr Calabash went on, still holding Miss Pink's hand, "is that Miss Pink and I are going to get married . . . and . . ."

He seemed to run out of words here, so Miss Pink took over.

"And we want you to know that we think of you, Chipo, Gentle and Dede, as our children."

Gentle's eyes filled with tears, and Dede smiled so much that Chipo thought his face might split. Chipo just stared at everyone around the table in turn, and decided he must be the luckiest person in the world.

Now that they really were a family, everyone began to think about the future. Dede, who had always imagined his career as a musician, began to plan for it. Once a week he took money to a music shop downtown, where he was paying for a guitar, bit by bit.

"I've only paid for the strings so far," he said, beaming. "But if we keep on making money like this I'll own the whole instrument by the time the rains are over!"

Having plans for his future made Dede feel a bit better about his past. One night, when they were all sitting cosily around the stove and the rain was beating on the tin roof, he told them how he'd ended up in Rubbish Town.

"My dad was a travelling tora player. He was always away. One time he went away and never came back. Mum had eight kids and I was the youngest. She sold me to this guy who got kids to work on dumps and in factories. But I was so small he couldn't get any money for me." Dede laughed. "I don't think Fudu paid much for me, but he still didn't get a bargain!" It was a sad story, but Dede had told it as if it was a big joke.

Miss Pink and Mr Calabash looked at each other over Dede's head, and Chipo saw their eyes glittering with tears. They didn't say anything, but when Dede went to bed, Miss Pink laid one of her shawls over him as he slept.

Gentle was planning too. She spent her money on embroidery thread. The little embroidered cloths she made sold well, and every night she sat under the lamp making more. She was saving up to go to school – as well as Happy Split-face Land.

"I'm going to be a doctor!" Chipo heard her whispering to Miss Pink one evening.

Gentle becoming a doctor! Chipo didn't say anything. Her crazy dreams were harmless enough; and anyway, pretty soon he'd have a bakery, so she could work there and be happy and forget all about school.

One day, on the way to work, he decided to ask Mr Atee to keep his saved money safe for him, instead of having it clinking around his middle like a belly made of coins.

"I will be your bank!" Mr Atee exclaimed. "You can write down how much I am keeping for you in this book, so you'll know I am not cheating you."

Chipo looked at Mr Atee. He didn't want to admit that he couldn't read or write, so he said, "It will be hard for me to count my money and write it all down at the same time."

Mr Atee understood at once. "So," he said, "*you* will count the money and *I* can write it down."

Chipo nodded and wondered, for the first time, if Gentle had been right all along about going to school. To be a think-quick, move-fast businessman you might have to read and write. But he pushed the thought to the back of his mind – going to school was as crazy as Happy Split-face Land.

When Chipo finished work, he counted up his money, and Mr Atee wrote the amount and the date in the back of his big green accounts book, then locked the cash away in his great fat safe. Chipo walked home with a much lighter heart and no clinking belly; he thought about how people would one day say, *That Chipo, he's a millionaire and he did it all without reading or writing!*

He was wondering how long it would take to save up enough money from Mouse's performances to set up his own bakery, when Dede and Gentle ran up to him, yelling, "Mouse is gone!"

Chapter 22

Inside the tin house on Rose Street everyone
was gathered around the stove, drinking
tea and telling Chipo the story of Mouse's
disappearance, like people running a relay race.

"I let her out when it got light, so she could
wee," Gentle explained. She was trying her
hardest to be brave, but Chipo saw her bottom
lip wobbling and her eyes glinting with the
tears she was doing her best to hold back.

"We heard her barking and growling,"
Dede added.

"She was making a big, big noise," said Mr Calabash, shaking his head, "so we all ran outside to see what was the matter . . ."

". . . and we saw two boys pull her into the back of a pick-up, with a sack over her head," Miss Pink concluded.

"It drove off so fast," said Dede. "I ran after it but I couldn't catch up."

No one seemed to know what to do or say. Chipo tried to think quick, but thinking slowly was all he could manage.

"I don't think Mouse will do tricks for anyone who put a sack over her head!" Gentle said defiantly.

Chipo looked at his sister. Why did she always think of things just the moment before he did? She was right. Mouse would bite and snarl, she wouldn't twirl and dance. And maybe the sort of people who stole dogs wouldn't want her to anyway.

At last his brain had a quick thought. The sort of people who stole valuable performing animals wanted to make money in a hurry. They would say, *You can have your dog back if you pay us lots of money*. He was sure he'd seen something on TV about a crime just like it.

"They haven't taken her to do tricks for them," he said. Three puzzled faces turned towards him; only Gentle understood – she looked at him and nodded her head.

Chipo continued, "The thieves will threaten to kill Mouse if we don't give them money!"

"Ah!" said Mr Calabash. "I have heard of this. It's called a ransom demand!"

"Yes, a ransom," agreed Miss Pink, getting quite excited. "That means Mouse has been kidnapped!"

"Dognapped," Dede corrected her, and

they might have laughed if they hadn't been so worried.

Everyone began talking at once. Mr Calabash said that they must stay calm and act as if it was a normal day so as not to give the dognappers any encouragement. Miss Pink said she'd like to show them a bit of encouragement with a very big stick on their backsides. Dede said he would give back all the parts of the guitar that he owned to get money for Mouse's ransom. Gentle said that she hoped Mouse was biting the thieves very hard. Chipo just kept saying that he had a plan, even though it wasn't fully formed; just something to do with Mouse always making that awful noise when she smelled Mr Atee's pastry. But nobody was listening anyway. And then, in the middle of all their chatter, there was a loud scraping at the tin house door as something was pushed underneath. Mr Calabash dashed outside, but all that could be seen of the "postman" was a small retreating figure and a pair of fast-pumping legs.

The something was a piece of thick cardboard that had been ripped from a box; it was about the size of a hand. Someone had written quite a few words on it in black biro. Mr Calabash picked it up.

"This is a ransom note!" he said as if his whole life had been spent dealing with dognappers and their demands.

"What does it say?" said Gentle.

"I . . . I . . . don't have the eyes for it . . ." he muttered, and handed the note to Miss Pink.

"Don't go on about your bad eyes, you old rogue," she scolded. "You never learned to read, and neither did I!"

She handed the note to Gentle and said sadly, "We have all been too busy surviving in this hard world to make time for learning!"

"And *we* can't read either," Gentle wailed. "So we can't help Mouse!" She stamped her foot and began to cry in anger and frustration. Even Chipo felt for the first time that things would have been better if someone could have read the note. He even thought it would be best if that someone could have been him. But there was no time for that now. He had to think like Powerbolt and make the best of a bad situation.

"Sending a ransom note that nobody can read isn't very clever," Chipo said, although that was mostly to make Gentle feel better. "These dognappers may be able to read but I think we're cleverer! I know how we're going to find Mouse and get her back."

Gentle's tears dried. She opened her mouth

to ask questions, but before she could get going Chipo put his hands on her shoulders and said, "I am Chipo Superhero, I have a plan. I will get Mouse back for you, little sister."

She gave him a soggy smile and nodded.

"You go with Mr Calabash and Miss Pink as usual, Gentle," Chipo told her. "Mr Calabash is right – we must show the thieves that we don't care what they do. Dede and I are going to Mr Atee's. And we have to go right now!"

Dede was small, but he could run almost as fast as Chipo, so they made good progress across town. They ran past their old courtyard, and then all the way up Palm Drive and across town on Freedom Drive. All the roads were busy and full of people, many of whom seemed to be moving house. Carts and rickety cars loaded with pots and pans, furniture and chickens were heading out of the city. For the first time in weeks there had been gunfire in the night, and two big explosions downtown. Chipo knew that this was a bad sign, a sign that something big and probably nasty was about to happen. He debated for a moment whether they should turn back, but it was his duty as a businessman to find Mouse: she made their family a lot of money. And even if Mouse had just been an ordinary dog, he had promised his little sister that he would find her. He would keep that promise!

They stopped for a moment to cross the main route north out of town, Umdebby Road, and more carts and cars loaded with household goods and grumbling children trundled past.

"What's going on, Chipo?" Dede asked. "Why are all these people leaving?"

"It doesn't matter what's going on," Chipo replied grimly. "We're getting Mouse back!"

But inside he felt uncertain, as if he might be about to do something very foolish.

They ran on, and between panting breaths Chipo explained his plan, which had crystallized in his head as they'd raced across town: first, Mr Atee was certainly able to read, so he could tell them what the ransom note said, which might help (although Chipo didn't really want to admit that reading was any sort of useful skill); second, Mr Atee would be about to do his delivery round, taking bread to little shops all over this part of the city; and third, Chipo and Dede would go too, with a big bag of pastry scraps. If Mouse smelled their irresistible smell, she would make the telltale wailing-howling-yowl noise, and Chipo and Dede would then know exactly where she was.

"Why can't we just call her name from Mr Atee's van?"

"Because the dognappers will hear us!"

"And what do we do when we've found her?"

This was the part of the plan that Chipo hadn't truly thought through, but he answered Dede confidently: "They won't be expecting us, so we can probably just rush in and grab her."

There was no time for more questions. They were almost at Mr Atee's. But as the two boys turned the corner into Astove Street, they saw that Mr Atee's van was loaded with the contents of his house and his three children, not loaves of bread ready for delivery. Mr Atee was just about to get in and drive away, but when he saw Chipo, he jumped down from the driver's seat.

"Chipo! I'm so glad to see you." He reached into his pocket, pulled out some bank notes and handed them over. "This is the money you left for me to take care of. Use it to get out."

If Mr Atee was going, perhaps things were

really bad; Chipo suddenly felt a bit dazed.

"But my dog's been stolen!" he found himself saying. "I need you to read this note."

Mr Atee looked at Chipo as if he were mad and pushed the note away with his hand. "Don't you know soldiers are coming?" he said. "A whole army! I must get my family out of the city, and you must leave too. Right now."

He climbed into the van and drove away, joining the long stream of other cars and carts.

"We must get back to the tin house and warn everyone," said Dede.

Chipo had forgotten about Dede. He looked down at him as if seeing him from a long way away. "You go," he told him. "I have to find Mouse."

For a moment Dede hesitated; then he patted Chipo's arm, as lightly as a leaf, and took to his heels.

Chapter 23

The ransom note didn't really matter, Chipo thought. Perhaps Mouse's captors had already decided to run away like Mr Atee, and wouldn't want the bother of a dog. And anyway, he was just going to find her and take her back to Gentle.

Chipo ran into the bakery. The tins he had cleaned earlier in the day were piled up ready for the next bake. Loaves were stacked on shelves ready to be delivered – Chipo put two into his bag as he guessed food might be hard to come by in the next few days. At the far end of the room was a whole tray of pastries, still warm and fragrant. Chipo found a flour sack and stuffed them into it. As they were crushed they released even more of their delicious smell. But Chipo didn't think of eating even a crumb: he was concentrating on his plan. He tied string to the sack to make it into a kind of backpack, and punched holes all over to let out the smell. Then he ran across to the shed in the corner of the yard. It was padlocked, but the door was so old and rickety it was easy to break down.

"Sorry, Mr Atee," Chipo breathed as he pulled Mr Atee's ancient bike from the back of the shed and rode off down the street.

He wove in and out of the cars and carts, the vans and lorries. Everywhere he went people turned to see where the delicious smell was coming from; despite the clouds of exhaust fumes and the hot smell of dust, Mr Atee's pastries sent out their silent call to anything living that had a nose and taste buds!

Chipo was pretty sure the dognappers were somewhere in the web of tiny streets between the Umdebby Road and the bottom of Palm Drive. He crossed the bustle of the Umdebby Road, now even more crammed with overloaded vehicles, and slipped into the maze of little side streets beyond – all too small to have names. Here, huts and compounds were built of tin and wood and scraps of polythene amongst the ruins and rubble left from the last time an army came through the city. Not many people were leaving from these back alleys. Either, like Chipo and his family, they hadn't heard the news that soldiers were coming, or they realized they weren't going to get very far with the only transport they had, which was their own feet. But they were staying inside their huts and compounds, so the streets were unusually empty, and people stared at Chipo from doorways.

The only living things on the street were stray dogs, and pretty soon Chipo had a string of them following behind, their noses glued to the pastry smell from the flour sack. But no telltale yowl came from behind anyone's fence as Chipo had imagined it would.

The longer he went on searching, the worse he felt. He thought about what Mr Atee had told him, and about the crowds leaving the city; he thought about the pictures on Gentle's bandage map and how Gentle had described them.

Here's the planes and the bombs, and here's everybody all dead, and here's you and me, running away, alive . . .

Suddenly he felt that the distance between him and his sister back at the tin house was too much to bear. His plan had been crazy, just like his plan to get the TV from the dump had been crazy. Mouse was gone; he would never get her back. He must return to Gentle, to Dede and Mr Calabash and Miss Pink. He tore the sack of pastries from his back and threw it down in the road, where the stray dogs fell on it, snarling at each other, and began to pedal towards the tin house as fast as he could. And at the very moment he gave up hope of Mouse and turned for home, her voice came wailing and yowling from behind a high corrugated tin fence almost beside him. Before he could stop himself, he'd answered her yowl.

"Mouse! Mouse!"

He was off the bike, running towards her. Now she'd heard him, Mouse barked

madly, and her claws scrabbled against
the metal that imprisoned her, but Chipo
couldn't hear any human voice telling her
to be quiet; the dognappers must be out –
perhaps fleeing the city or even delivering
another useless ransom note.

Chipo ran round the outside of the fence
as quietly as he could, trying to find the way
in, but there didn't seem to be any entrance
or break in the solid sheet of ridged metal.
And then he tripped and fell flat; his foot had
caught on a metal ring in the ground. He
pulled it, and the dust fell from a trapdoor
leading into a dark tunnel that had to be the
entrance to Mouse's prison. He dropped down
into it, shutting the trapdoor behind him so
if the thieves returned they wouldn't realize at
once that something was wrong.

Inside was a yard and a roofed compound

with bedding and clothes lying tossed about. It looked like the thieves hadn't planned to be gone for long. They might return at any minute – which meant that Chipo and Mouse were in danger. Chipo knew he had to be quick.

Mouse was chained to a pole in the yard, the bag still over her head. Chipo took it off and freed her from the choke chain around her neck. Immediately she became calm, and laid her big heavy head in his hands with a little "*Uff-uff!*" of gratitude. For a moment Chipo looked into the dog's green spangled eyes and realized he had been wrong to think that Mouse only really cared for Gentle. He stroked her good ear.

"Come on, Mouse," he said. "Let's go!"

But on the other side of the metal wall he heard whispering voices and the sound of the trapdoor being lifted. The thieves were back and they knew something was wrong. If they found him here now, he was trapped, and he and Mouse would probably both be killed and the money stripped out of his back pocket. They had less than seconds to escape, but how?

"Jump, Mouse! Jump!" Chipo commanded her.

Perhaps it was the lingering smell of Mr Atee's pastry coming from the other side of the wall, but Mouse cleared it in one leap, her highest ever. Chipo pulled at the pole she'd been tied to with all his might, and as the end came free, he ran and pole-vaulted over the wall after her.

By the time the dognappers had found that their compound was indeed entirely empty of any sort of dog or human, Chipo was racing into town on Mr Atee's bike with Mouse bounding joyfully beside him.

But they were by no means out of danger, and Chipo knew it. Dark clouds were gathering for the afternoon rains, and the sickening drone of aeroplanes rolled under them, more ominous than thunder. Before they reached their old courtyard, the planes had begun to drop their bombs on the city.

Chapter 24

When a bomb blew up the road in front of them, Chipo and Mouse jumped into a ditch. It was wet and full of rubbish, but it gave them some protection. Chipo lay with his arms around Mouse and his face buried in her furry side. And as the bombs hit the ground with their sickening *thwump, thwump*, he remembered all he'd thought he'd forgotten about the day when he and Gentle had lost their family . . .

. . . *the planes had droned overhead just as they did now, and the bombs had hit the ground with the same sound. There had been gunfire too; the bullets had zipped past him like wasps as he clung to his mother's back. She was running, but then she fell and lay still and wouldn't answer him. She was lying on his leg, and his leg hurt and he couldn't get up; he called out to her, but she still didn't hear. Then someone came and pulled him free and carried him on their back, because he was too small to walk. And the someone wasn't Azi or Darren or Patience, but Gentle, the sister with the split face who he'd always been a little scared of. She comforted him and carried him away, and told him in her funny way of speaking, "I'm your big sister, Chipo. I'll take care of you."*

And that was just what she had been doing, every time she called him Big Brother and let

him believe he was the older one who was taking
care of her.

The bombs had stopped. Chipo and Mouse
crawled out of the ditch. In the road there was
a huge hole where Mr Atee's bike had been.
It began to rain – just a few fat drops at first,
splashing into the dust, and then sheets and
curtains of it, washing Chipo and Mouse clean
as they walked.

Bombs had fallen everywhere, and blown
whole streets into nothing but dust and scraps.
It looked, Chipo thought, like the dump.

The world had gone quiet. Their footsteps
made no noise, the rain fell without a sound,
and even the lightning that cracked across the
sky had no thunder to accompany it. In this
new quiet world, all Chipo could hear was his
own heart, pounding out a rhythm of fear:

fear that he would never see Gentle or Dede or Miss Pink or Mr Calabash again, and that once again bombs had blown his family apart.

Chipo began to run, his feet splashing soundlessly through the puddles, his heart beating. He ran down what had been Palm Drive, and through their old courtyard, now just a space filled with rubble and the blackened remains of the tree that had given them shade. He reached Rose Street, and the place where the tin house had stood, but there was nothing around him but flattened ruins. He stood there in the rain, bewildered, and then noticed that someone was pulling on his hand and shouting into his face.

It was Dede, standing in front of him with blood and tears trickling down his face.

With a great rush that made his legs wobble, sound and reality returned to Chipo. He

swallowed hard and asked the question, dreading
the answer that might come: "Where's Gentle?"

Dede didn't seem to have heard him.
"A bomb fell," he said, pointing wildly.
"Over there. No, there . . Somewhere
near . . . and . . ."

"Where's Gentle?" Chipo asked again.

"The house fell on us; other stuff fell on us. Then Miss Pink, Mr Calabash – they went out to look for you." Dede's eyes were open very wide, and his whole body shook.

Chipo put his hands on Dede's shoulders and held him steady. He asked again, "Where is Gentle?"

At last Dede understood the question. He stopped shaking and his eyes looked at Chipo properly. "She was hurt when the house fell," he explained.

"But she's alive!"

"Yes, yes," said Dede. "She's alive. An ambulance came. Doctors. They took her to the hospital outside the city. The Memorial Hospital, they said . . ."

Chipo found he was gulping air with relief. Maybe the bombs hadn't destroyed everything this time; he had Mouse and he had Dede; he would find Miss Pink and Mr Calabash. He would. But later. Right now he would go to his sister.

"How bad is your cut, Dede?" Chipo asked. "Can you walk far?"

"It's just a scratch on my head," he said, smiling and doing a lame little dance on the spot. "I can walk miles!"

"Good, then let's put a string around Mouse's neck and get to the hospital!"

While Dede found a string lead for Mouse, Chipo scratched a message for Miss Pink and Mr Calabash on one of the fallen tin walls of their house: a box with a big cross in to show the hospital, with an arrow pointing to it to show that was where they had gone; beside that three stick children, a stick man, a stick woman, and a huge stick dog, under the roof of a house, all together.

Chapter 25

Everyone who hadn't left before the bombs fell was trying to leave now, so there were all kinds of cars and carts, trucks and pick-ups heading out of the city. Chipo showed a truck driver one of the notes that Mr Atee had given him, to pay for their ride out to the hospital, and Mouse showed him her teeth to tell him that was all they would pay. Then the two boys and their big dog climbed onto the top of the truck, as the inside was already full of people and their bundles of belongings.

Neither boy had been to the hospital before, but it was pretty easy to spot – a huge complex of five big buildings, each four storeys high. There was a stream of ambulances and other cars and trucks carrying people who'd been hurt in the bombing to its gates. There were hundreds of people on foot too, trudging up the road and waiting in a crowd outside the hospital doors.

The boys climbed a tree to get a better look at the situation, leaving Mouse yowling for them at the bottom. It didn't look any more hopeful from a height; however were they going to find one small girl in that great unhappy sea of humans? Then Dede pointed at something.

"Look!" he said. "Up there – the middle floor of the third building. Look!" He was so excited he almost fell out of the tree.

Chipo looked to where the last rays of the

evening sun were slanting under the cloud and lighting up the dirty grey face of the hospital. A pale, tattered piece of material was dangling from a window and flapping in the breeze. Even from this distance you could see that it was covered with little black marks. It was Gentle's bandage and, just like the map it was meant to be, it was showing them exactly where to go.

The boys scrambled down and wriggled their way through the crowds to the hospital gates, where two very large and serious-looking guards stood at a barrier inspecting people before letting them pass. As the boys and Mouse approached, one of the men held up a large hand.

"No dogs!" he said.

"She's a performing dog," said Chipo. "She's special."

"A dog," said the man, "is a dog, and you cannot bring a dog onto hospital property."

The solution was clear: Dede should stay with Mouse while Chipo went inside, as they couldn't risk leaving Mouse tied up alone. But neither of them liked the idea of being separated, even for a short time, while their family was already in so many pieces and the possibility of more bombs, guns and soldiers was real and close. They stood together like a little island with people slowly flowing around them, until Chipo said, "Wait by the tree we climbed, and I'll come and find you."

"OK," said Dede, very uncertainly. "Will you come back?"

"Yes, Dede," said Chipo solemnly. "I will come back. I might be a long time, but wait. Just wait. I will come back, and then we'll work out how to find Miss Pink and Mr Calabash."

"I'll wait," agreed Dede. "Tell Gentle I said get better soon."

Alone, Chipo moved much more quickly through the crowds. He was soon past the guards and standing in front of a desk where several harassed-looking ladies were dealing with the hundreds of patients and their relatives.

"I've come to see my sister," Chipo explained to one of them, whose name badge said MRS BAH. "She's in the middle building on the third floor." He used his most charming calabash-selling voice.

Mrs Bah didn't even look at him. "She can't be. That's the special surgery ward. What's her name?"

"Gentle."

"Gentle what?"

"Um . . . just Gentle."

"What is her family name?"

"We haven't got a family name."

The woman looked up at him crossly.

"You are wasting my time, little boy. Go away."
She turned to help the next person.

Chipo was pushed against a wall by the
press of people. If Gentle wasn't on the third
floor of the middle building, where was she?
And why did they need to know what his
family was called when he didn't even know
it himself? Chipo was ready to cry with
frustration. Supposing Gentle died before he
got to her? Supposing he never found her?

No – he wouldn't let that happen; he would
search every part of the hospital until he *did*
find her, and he'd start just where her map had
told him to!

He dodged past the front desk and Mrs Bah
and her helpers, hidden by a forest of taller
adults, and ran down a long corridor so fast
that the guard didn't even see him. At the end
of the building was a door, and Chipo ran out

into the dark and along the outside of the next building to the third one. Round the back was an open door, then an empty corridor. Chipo walked down it, looking for a quiet staircase where no one would notice him slipping up to the third floor.

But the only staircase was at the front of the building, and it was far from quiet. Patients were being carried down on stretchers, or walking with the help of nurses or relatives, out into the dark where two big buses waited to take them. Doctors and guards stood around shouting instructions, and no one took the slightest notice of Chipo, even when he began to dodge and weave his way up the stairs between all those who were coming down.

It took a lot of concentration to keep out of the way of the stretchers and medical equipment and still make progress upwards, but at last he reached the third floor.

It echoed with emptiness and silence. Gentle had been moved along with all the other patients. Outside, Chipo heard one of the buses driving away and ran to the window. There, tied to the frame, was Gentle's bandage. He leaned out to pull it in, and as he did so, a little voice called up to him from down below.

"Theepo! Theepo!" And there was Gentle, waiting on the tarmac to be loaded into the bus.

"Hurry, Chipo, hurry," she called. "I've got to go!"

Chapter 26

Getting back down the stairs was like running in a nightmare where your legs work their hardest but you stand still. On the last flight Chipo jumped over the banister and let himself drop into the hall so he could race through the doors and outside.

Gentle was still there, lying on a stretcher with a tube coming out of one arm. Large patches of blood showed through the white dressings on her other arm and both her legs. She looked very tiny. As Chipo reached her, two men picked up her stretcher and began to head for the bus, so he had to run beside to keep up.

"Where are they taking you?" he asked her.

Gentle was sleepy and weak, but she laughed softly when he asked this question. "To Happy Split-face Land, Chipo," she said. "It's a real place where doctors mend split faces. The doctors want to mend my face because they have never seen one split so bad. Then I won't have a split face any more. Imagine that, Chipo! I will be just like other people."

No, Chipo thought, *you will never, never, never be like other people. No one is as strong as you. And now you are leaving me, and I can't even tell you how strong I know you are, my big sister*. But he didn't say it. Instead he asked, "But where is this place?"

"It is very far," said Gentle sadly. "Very far.

In England. Here, the doctor wrote it for me —
this is where I will be."

She pulled a scrap of paper from inside her
white hospital shirt and gave it to him. It was
covered in words and letters.

"But I can't read!" Chipo almost wailed.

Gentle smiled and brushed his arm with
her fingers. "Then think quick, move fast, big
brother," she said, "and learn, so you can find
me! I know we will find each other."

They'd reached the bus and the men carried
Gentle inside. Chipo wanted to shout that
he knew he was not her big brother, that she
was his big sister and he didn't know what he
would do without her. But he knew that if
he did, no matter how sick she was, or how
much she wanted her split face to be mended,
Gentle would just get off the bus and stay with
him. So he kept quiet, and made stupid faces

through the glass that separated them, until Gentle's head nodded and she fell asleep.

Chipo felt a hand on his shoulder. It was one the stretcher bearers.

"Don't worry – the doctors have given her medicine to make her sleep on the journey," he said, and then added in a whisper, "But if you like, you could go with her. Just get in while no one is paying attention. But you must be quick – we're leaving right now."

Chipo looked up at Gentle's sleeping face. At last she was going to Happy Split-face Land, the real place, where she'd always wanted to be. The face that had been such a trial to her, that had made her ill, that had made her an outcast, would finally be healed. And Gentle was strong. She didn't need his help any more. But Dede and Mouse, Miss Pink and Mr Calabash needed someone who could think quick and move fast; a superhero better than Powerbolt, a real live big brother, a real live son.

"Thank you," Chipo answered, "but the rest of my family need me here. When she wakes up, tell her she'll see her big brother again soon. And give her this." He pulled Gentle's bandage out of his pocket, where he had shoved it to run back down the stairs.

"What is this?"

"She'll tell you," said Chipo.

The man smiled and nodded. He got onto the bus, and Chipo watched as it pulled away into the dark.

Dede and Mouse were still under the tree, and as Chipo got closer he could see that Miss Pink and Mr Calabash were there too; they had understood his sign and had come to find them. He tucked the paper with Gentle's destination written on it safely into his pocket, and then he walked back out through the gates to where his family were waiting for him.

Epilogue

Chipo asked the driver to drop him at the clinic outside town.

"You are a doctor, then?" the driver asked, smiling.

"No, no! I'm a teacher."

As Chipo got off the bus, the driver called after him, "Goodbye, teacher! Go well!"

He waved back, then zipped the book he'd been reading on the journey into his bag and checked for the millionth time that he had brought the photos: of his graduation, of his pupils in Rubbish Town looking just like he and his sister used to look; of Dede's band on stage; of Miss Pink's wedding to Mr Calabash; and the old faded one of Mouse and her pups. So many things had happened – a whole fifteen years had passed. They'd been separated by wars and oceans and continents; had lost each other entirely for a while. But now they were both found, and Chipo knew that as soon as he saw his sister, all those years would fall away and wouldn't matter at all.

Round a bend in the road he got his first sight of the neat, white-walled clinic. He was so close now. His heart was beating wildly, so he stopped and looked around to try to calm himself. The first rains had come and the land was green again. Fresh grass covered the low hills like a fuzz of velvet, and the thorn trees were yellow with blossom. A group of birds –

bee-eaters, he thought – swooped through the sunlight over a puddle in the road. As a child in the dump and in the city, he'd never realized that his country was so beautiful. *This*, he thought, *this beauty is what I want every child I teach to know*.

Chipo looked back towards the clinic. A small figure in a white doctor's coat was walking along the road towards him. She was coming out to meet him. In his excitement he'd forgotten she'd said she would. She held something above her head, and the breeze caught it, unravelling it like a banner. Even from this distance he knew the story its stitched pictures told. Gentle would have filled in all the gaps.

About the author . . .

Nicola Davies graduated from Cambridge with
a degree in zoology before going on to become
a writer and presenter of radio and television
programmes such as THE REALLY WILD SHOW.
Amongst her many acclaimed books for children
are *Big Blue Whale*, *One Tiny Turtle*, *Ice Bear*,
Extreme Animals and *Poo*, which was shortlisted for
a Blue Peter Book Award. Her novel *Home* was
shortlisted for the Branford Boase award.

A Girl Called Dog

*Dog wasn't really a dog, she was a human girl.
But she was called Dog because that is what
Uncle had always called her.*

Shy, quiet Dog has never talked to another person,
and has to live in Uncle's pet shop with the animals
– her only friends. But one day a mysterious parcel
arrives: Carlos the parrot, a chattering bundle of
colour, feathers and incredible stories.

Suddenly Dog has a chance to escape. Along with
Carlos and her best friend, Esme the coati, Dog sets
off on a scary, exciting adventure. But can brave
Carlos help Dog find her voice at last?

**Longlisted for the UKLA Children's Book Award;
shortlisted for the Leicester Book Award, the
Portsmouth Book Award and the Stockton
Children's Book of the Year.**

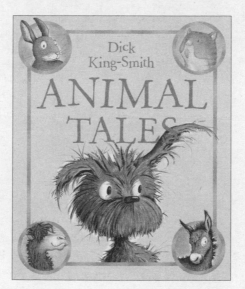

Michael Morpurgo

THE LAST WOLF

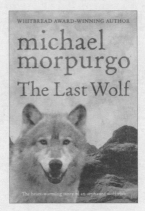

'I shall call you Charlie, for you are bonnie and a prince among wolves.'

When Robbie McLeod finds an orphaned wolf cub and vows to take care of him, it is the beginning of an adventure that sweeps boy and beast from the Highlands to the high seas and beyond.

Award-winning author Michael Morpurgo creates a spellbinding story of bravery and loyalty, brought vividly to life by Michael Foreman's stunning illustrations.